THE OTHER ALICE

Other books by Julia Clarke

Between You and Me
Chasing Rainbows
Summertime Blues
You Lose Some, You Win Some

THE OTHER ALICE

JULIA CLARKE

OXFORD
UNIVERSITY PRESS

OXFORD
UNIVERSITY PRESS

Great Clarendon Street, Oxford OX2 6DP

Oxford University Press is a department of the University of Oxford.
It furthers the University's objective of excellence in research, scholarship,
and education by publishing worldwide in

Oxford New York

Auckland Cape Town Dar es Salaam Hong Kong Karachi
Kuala Lumpur Madrid Melbourne Mexico City Nairobi
New Delhi Shanghai Taipei Toronto

With offices in
Argentina Austria Brazil Chile Czech Republic France Greece
Guatemala Hungary Italy Japan Poland Portugal Singapore
South Korea Switzerland Thailand Turkey Ukraine Vietnam

Oxford is a registered trade mark of Oxford University Press
in the UK and in certain other countries

British Library Cataloguing in Publication Data

Data available

ISBN-13: 978-0-19-275415-8
ISBN-10: 0-19-275415-7

3 5 7 9 10 8 6 4 2

Typeset in Meridien by
Palimpsest Book Production Limited,
Polmont, Stirlingshire
Printed in Great Britain by Cox and Wyman,
Reading, Berkshire

*This book is dedicated to Liz Cross with love
and many thanks for her help.*

Chapter 1

Mabel's a bitch and she's in a terrible mood. An 'I'm in season—don't mess with me'-type strop. The weather is bizarre. During the last month of school there was a heatwave (having exams in the main hall was like being microwaved). And, since we broke up, every day seems to get hotter. Dad has been going on for years about turning off lights because of global warming—and it seems that he might have been right all along.

The extreme heat makes Mabel irritable. It makes me irritable too. Gramps's old house is made of stone and is normally cool, but most of the windows have been sealed up for years by ancient coats of paint and today the ones that are open let in only warm air that smells of pigs. By midday the house seems to vibrate with heat and stickiness and the buzz of wasps trapped against glass.

Mabel begins to whine and scratch at the back door. I am meant to be clearing up—hoovering and dusting and all that stuff—because Mum is coming home. But it's just too hot. I am also meant to be helping Gary (Gramps's only employee) in the shop. But when I went in there Gary was staring morosely at the back page of the *Sun*. Even in this weather he wears his beanie hat pulled down over his eyes and a lumberjack shirt. He said there were no customers and he didn't need a hand. It all made me feel so depressed I watched TV for ages.

And now Mabel wants to go out. Before we can leave I have to do a recce around the house in case the collie from the farm down the lane is waiting to ambush her. Last night he staked out the front door and howled at the moon. He seems to sense that the days of her attraction are nearly over and is getting desperate.

There is no sign of the collie. 'Come on, Mabs,' I say kindly. 'We'll sneak out and walk down to the river, keep you out of trouble.'

Gramps has promised that one day Mabel will have proper pups from a stud dog and, when that happens, I can have one for my very own. I take it as a great compliment that Gramps has asked me to look after Mabel. So I'm not going to let her get caught out by any scruffy old sheepdog—even if she does have the hots for him.

Mabel does a runner as soon as I open the back door. She jerks the lead from my fingers and is off. I try calling her nicely. I try a cross voice. But nothing works. All I can do is chase after her shouting like a lunatic. Gary is still engrossed in the *Sun* and doesn't even glance up as I race by. Apart from him there's only a herd of Friesian cows and some fat saddleback pigs to hear me. There are some advantages to being stuck in the middle of nowhere.

Mabel—infuriatingly—doesn't take any of our normal routes, neither does she make for the shady trees and cool grey waters of the river. Instead she sets off for the crag and the dark woods at the back of the house. She's been trying to get up there for ages. Last thing at night, when the gate is closed, I always take her out into the garden for a sniff around and a wee. And, for the past week, she has rushed to the end of the garden and barked up at the crag. I have started to wonder if a feral cat is living there among the dark stones and that's why she goes so crazy. And today, it seems, she has turned into Mabel—cat-killer.

'Mabel! Come back!' I wail in panic. I hate the crag and the dark woods. When I was younger, Nell and Ed used to sneak me up there—although we were strictly forbidden to climb the rocks. I never go there now. I hate the place.

But I have no choice. Either Mabel's hormones are raging and she has arranged to meet the collie at a lovers' rendezvous—or she's got the scent of a cat living near her patch and is going to sort it. Either way, I've got to catch her.

Reluctantly, I follow her into the dark wood. It's a dismal place: full of huge old trees, rotting debris, and leaf mould so thick it is like cushions under my feet. The light is dim and dusty—heavy as soup with spores and pollen. The dampness and half-light feeds strange fungi and the stench of dead things rises in a fog around me.

3

'Mabel, come back,' I yell. 'I'm not going all the way to the top of the bloody crag!'

Buttersyke Crag rises from the top of the hill like a clenched fist threatening the sky and Mabel is making straight for the summit. She's on a mission. And I fear that she has been bewitched by last night's full moon, the collie, and the idea of puppies wriggling in her belly. Oh, hell . . .

I catch up with her right at the very top. I've had to avoid fallen branches, holly, and brambles—so I am scratched and breathless when I burst into the sunlight.

Mabel stands on the crest of the very highest rock. Her nose is up—her tail down. She's poised like a stag at bay.

'Mabel, Mabel, sweetheart,' I plead. Running so hard uphill has made my legs go weak. And, as I search the pockets of my shorts for a dog biscuit, my hands are shaking. Partly it's exhaustion, but it's also fear. I have such bad memories of Ed and Nell bringing me up here when I was a little kid. They were so horrible to me. They would tease me with stupid stories about bad men and boast that they could jump from ridiculous heights. It all seems a long time ago now, but what pisses me off is that I am still frightened. It is as if someone or something is watching me.

'Mabel, come here . . . please . . . please . . .' I beg. But Mabel takes no notice of my tearful voice. With a bark she leaps off the rock and dives into the undergrowth below.

4

I race to the place where she disappeared—but the top of the crag is so high all I can see is tree tops. I try to follow her—but my two legs are no match for her four. Halfway down the slope I lose my footing and slide and bump my way down through the under-growth to where the ground levels off. I have landed on the ledge that overlooks Gramps's garden and greenhouses. Nell and Ed used to call it the jumping stones—claiming that from here they could launch themselves off and land in Gramps's apple tree . . . as if.

My head is spinning and my stomach is in knots. I am just about as upset and cross as it is possible to be without actually screaming. 'Mabel,' I call out—my voice squeaky with panic and pain. I can hear her barking and I stand up unsteadily and turn to find her.

Mabel is standing guard under a small crooked oak tree that is rooted into the side of the stones. She is barking like a rabid wolf—going really mental.

And then I see why. Hanging in the tree above her is a red shape. I see the curves of a body. I see the colour of blood. My own blood is drumming in my ears, pumped by a wave of fear. The red thing is flut-tering like a flag. I sit down again abruptly and close my eyes. I don't want to look any more.

Chapter 2

It's a dress. It is on a hanger fastened to a branch. If I hadn't been so frightened and shaken up I would have known straight away that it wasn't substantial enough to be a body. But even so I am weak from the shock of seeing it hanging there.

'Mabel,' I croak. Mabel has given up barking and is eating something she has found on the ground. I could easily be dying but she appears not to have noticed.

'Mabel,' I say pathetically, hoping she will respond to my tearful voice. But she ignores me. It is sickening because Lassie was never like this. She helped total strangers when they were in trouble.

'Mabel!' I shout. 'Leave that alone, you disgusting animal!' I heave myself back onto my feet and rush over to her. It's the twins' birthday party tonight and Mum is coming back from Italy. The last thing I need is Mabel eating filth and throwing up—or worse—all over the kitchen floor.

When I get hold of Mabel's lead I have time to puzzle over the redness hanging in the tree. It is a sparkly designer evening dress—size 10. Then I spot a small tent hidden under the oak tree—it is tied up so I can't see inside, but all around it are half-eaten sandwiches, Coke cans, and cig ends—yuck!

'Come away,' I say urgently to Mabel. I am getting seriously scared again. I really don't like this place and I don't like the fact that some weirdo is camping here. But Mabel has got her nose glued to the ground. A tinker's den with food scraps is just her sort of place.

'Come on, you greedy pig,' I say crossly to her. And I pull at her lead until she follows me. I turn and walk to the edge of the ledge. I have this crazy idea that we might be able to scramble down and end up in Gramps's garden.

The sheer drop comes so suddenly that I nearly walk off the edge. Below me are the roofs of Gramps's cottage and the greenhouses. But there is no way anyone but Spider-Man could climb down from here. I feel trapped. In front of me is a precipice; behind me the dress and the campsite. My heart is thudding as I turn back to face the red dress. I am desperate to get away.

'Come on,' I whisper to Mabel. 'We'll have to climb back up to the crag and go through the woods. I want to get home,' I add, and my voice ends in a little sob. And Mabel, as if she can smell my fear, begins to run, tugging me upwards with her big strong shoulders. And so we clamber back up the slope together.

Because I am so panicky I run all the way home and make it back in record time. What should have been a walk in the sunshine turned into something like the opening scene of a horror film. The red dress and the squalid little campsite have really spooked me.

Mabel starts to bark and I stare at the clock unable to believe so much time has passed. It's as if I've been caught in a time warp. I look around the kitchen with despair and, for a split second, I consider trying to clear the table. But I realize it is no use. Nell is right outside the back door. I can hear her ordering Ed about. I sit down at the table and decide to tough it out.

I'm actually pretty angry with them because of how they used to terrorize me up at the crag. No wonder I don't like heights and hate flying. And, because of this, I am almost pleased (in some weird sado-masochistic way) that I haven't done what I was told to do. We'll all be pissed off now, won't we?

Nell walks into the kitchen and explodes like a box of fire crackers hurled into a bonfire. She has a short fuse at the best of times and the stress of throwing a big party at Gramps's house has sent her right over the edge. Even so, I am shocked at how she goes off.

'Oh-my-god-you-little-slut!' she screams. 'You haven't even cleared the breakfast things. How could you? When you know it's our party tonight. The caterers will be here soon. What on earth have you been doing?'

'I've been busy . . .' I say. 'I took Mabel for a walk,' I add lamely, my courage dwindling in the face of her outrage.

'Calm down, sis,' Ed says in a conciliatory tone from the doorway. 'We'll soon get cleared up.'

This is like chucking a petrol bomb onto the fire.

8

Nell flares up immediately. 'You've been busy?' she shrieks at me in disbelief. 'You don't know the meaning of the word. You are the laziest, most useless . . .' She picks up the packet of Weetabix and hurls it at my head. This isn't a clever move on her part because the inner bag hasn't been folded and Weetabix falls out onto the floor. Mabel is on a light diet because of her weight and she hasn't seen Weetabix since she was a little puppy. This is like manna from heaven to her and she does piggy snorts in her haste to eat it all up double-quick—as if Nell and I will fall on all fours and demand a share.

'Now look what you've done. She's not meant to have cereal!' I say to Nell.

'Get that revolting bloody animal out of the kitchen!' Nell yells in reply. 'It's a health hazard.'

'She's not a revolting bloody animal,' I say, stung. 'She's Gramps's dog and she has as much right to be in this house as you do—probably more. Gramps asked me to look after her—and that's what I'm doing.'

'The caterers will not want to work with an animal in the kitchen,' Nell says through gritted teeth.

'Caterers?' I echo. 'I thought it was Mrs Black and Dot from the pub coming up to make sandwiches. Anyway, they have a cat in the pub that sits on the worktops and licks the butter if it isn't kept covered. I know that for a fact.'

'Oh, shut up, you idiot,' Nell says dismissively. 'You always spoil everything, don't you?'

'No I don't,' I say, hurt. For as long as I can remember, the twins, and especially Nell, have complained that I spoil their fun—the truth is they never wanted a little sister. If I had arrived from a mail order catalogue they would have sent me back. 'It's you that spoils things, always picking on me,' I add.

And at that moment a wave of resentment hits me hard. I had thought I would keep quiet about going to the crag today. I certainly don't want to talk about finding the red dress. But remembering how horrible they were to me when I was little has rattled my bars. I blurt out angrily: 'You've always been mean to me. It's your fault I'm afraid of heights. I went to the jumping stones today.'

Behind me I hear the sounds of Ed depositing stuff for the party onto the worktop.

'What are you going on about?' Nell snaps.

'You used to take me up to the crag—even though we weren't allowed. Then you used to bully me.'

The details of what I remember flows out of me in a big gabble. 'You used to lean over me and say: "There's a wicked ugly old tramp living in this wood. The awful smell is his socks and yucky underpants. Be very quiet or he will hear us. If he jumps out we will have to run away . . ."' My voice, mimicking Nell's silky tone, drops to a malevolent whisper. '"Do you think you will be able to keep up with us? You're not very good at running, are you?"'

'Oh, don't be so pathetic,' Nell says dismissively.

'Do try to start behaving as if you are at secondary school—please.'

'You used to drag me from the crag down to that ledge and tell me I would have to leap off if the tramp came after us. You said you and Ed could jump all the way down to Gramps's garden and it was easy. You used to tell me that the horrible old tramp would eat me up and spit out my wellingtons. And I was so scared I used to pee my pants.' The humiliation of admitting that makes me want to cry.

Nell shrugs and laughs, as if to say: 'So what?'—but I sense she is embarrassed by this disclosure. In the background I can hear Ed laughing.

'You were such a bitch,' I say bitterly.

'Oh, do stop all this stupidity,' Nell says impatiently. 'Spence will think you're not right in the head.'

I am frozen by this remark. Shocked that someone has witnessed us behaving so badly: spitting like a pair of cats and throwing food. And that it should be Spence—her new boyfriend, the one she has been yakking on about for weeks—is doubly shocking.

I am mortified. Spence is bound to be one of Nell's snotty, up-himself friends and he has been listening to me recounting the traumas of my early childhood in graphic detail—right down to my wet knickers. My face flames at the thought. All I can do is to mutter: 'Oh, shut up,' to Nell. I can hear how childish and stupid I sound.

I stand up and turn around slowly. The first thing

I register is that Ed and Spence are both laughing at me. Then surprise takes over any other feeling because this Spence isn't anything like the guys that normally hang around Nell. He isn't at all good-looking or trendy. And he doesn't have dyed hair or designer stubble. In fact he's drop-dead ordinary and is wearing what Nell calls dismissively 'supermarket togs'—cheap chain-store jeans and T-shirt.

He's still laughing—he can't hide it—although he does try to straighten his face. 'Sorry to laugh,' he says. 'But that was very funny.'

'Well, it wasn't funny at the time and it was all true,' I say indignantly. I half expect him to turn away from me as I speak. Nell's friends normally treat me like a leper. To my astonishment, he not only looks into my eyes but gives me a lovely smile and says very seriously:

'It was very funny and very sad at the same time. And I don't doubt that it was true. The best humour generally is.' He says this to me as if we are having a proper grown-up conversation! And the fact that he is taking me seriously calms me right down—although I do look hard at him just in case he's taking the mick.

My first impression had been that he was just about the ugliest boy in the world: too tall, too bony, gaunt shoulders, and a nose that is way too big. But suddenly he doesn't seem ugly to me any more. In fact, he reminds me of some kind of extinct bird: a gentle creature that isn't frightened of humans, with a big beak, huge wing span, and kind eyes.

As I watch him I see his face change. His eyes stop twinkling and become troubled. His expression is full of concern. He moves across to me and says: 'Little sister—you're in the wars. What on earth have you been up to? You didn't really jump off those rocks at the back of the house, did you?'

He's really frowning, and he hunkers down with surprising grace and peers hard at my bare knees. I begin to blush. I stare down at his bent head: brown hair—quite curly. Nell hates curly hair on guys, but I think it's lovely.

I am embarrassed because I have been staring at him so hard and I glance down at my legs. I am shocked! One of my knees is covered in dirt and blood and there are quite a few rivulets of dried blood dribbling down into my trainer. It's gross. I don't know why Spence seems so enthralled by it—unless he is considering a career in medicine.

'That's a really nasty cut,' he says.

'Do stop fussing, it's only a scratch,' Nell calls out dismissively. She hasn't even looked. If I hobbled in with one leg missing she'd probably dismiss it as a minor injury.

She adds more sharply, 'Stop being such an attention-seeker. There's some Dettol in the cloak-room cupboard. Go and have a wash. You look like a tramp.'

Spence smiles up at me. 'Want me to sort it out for you? I think you've maybe got some grit in there. I'll try not to hurt you. I'm brilliant at first aid. I am

13

coach for the under-12s footie team that my brother's in. Tell you what, after all the practice I've had, I could turn Elastoplasts and Tubi-grip into an art form.'

There is such kindness in his expression that it gives me quite a lump in my throat and a burning of tears behind my eyes. I am suddenly aware of all the pain in my body: my aching muscles, all the cuts and scratches and sore skin. His pity has unlocked it all.

I bite my lip and shake my head. He rises to his feet and says: 'OK then, but make sure you get that cut really clean, won't you?' He dips his head so he can look into my eyes again as he says that. Then he turns away. It's all over in an instant.

I go into the cloakroom and run some hot water in the sink. I take a deep breath, soak my skinned hands and rub soap into them. It stings like mad for a split second and then, miraculously, I hardly notice. I scrub my knee; the grit is like sandpaper—and I don't feel that either. I am too swept up in all the emotions that are flooding over me—all other sensations are lost.

Then I go into denial. I tell myself that Nell's friends are always stuck-up and this Spence is no exception. I try to remember how he laughed at me—but can remember only his sympathy. I tell myself that he is ugly—but can recall only his smiling eyes and soft brown hair. I tell myself that he looks like a dodo— all bony with a long neck and a big nose. But it's no use. It just doesn't matter to me what he looks like.

To me he is the loveliest person in the whole world. It's weird—really, really strange.

The nearest experience I can relate it to was when I fell out of the apple tree in Gramps's garden. One minute I was in the branches calling out to Dad and waving, the next I was flat on my back on the grass, winded and gasping for breath. I had no memory of the seconds when I was falling. And this is the same. In the past all Nell's friends seemed hateful. But suddenly Spence seems totally perfect.

I am lost in a jumble of feeling that I don't understand. Just like when I fell through time and space and lost a couple of seconds of my life, I don't know what has happened to me. I just know I am different. A different me in a different world and there is no going back. I wouldn't go back—even if there was the remotest chance of turning back time and un-living those first moments of meeting Spence I wouldn't do it. I don't care about anything. I just want to see and speak to him again.

Chapter 3

I stay in the cloakroom for ages—too scared to leave. When I finally emerge to find Spence on his own in the kitchen I am so relieved my knees go weak.

'You and me got volunteered to clear up the kitchen,' he says with a grin. Then he adds kindly. 'I've made you a mug of tea with plenty of honey in it. It's good for shock.'

I suppose he's talking about my cut knee. Whereas right now the big shock for me is how I feel about him.

'Oh, thanks,' I say. There is a long silence between us. And I sip the tea until it's all gone even though it's disgusting. I can't think of a single thing to say. Being with him seems to wipe everything from my mind like a damp cloth on a marker board. The only sound in the kitchen is a gentle snoring from Mabel, who is stretched out under the table sleeping off her Weetabix meal. Her stomach is distended and I just have to pray that the Weetabix doesn't have a laxative effect.

Spence is busy. He's bent over the sink scrubbing at a particularly nasty casserole dish that dates from the last time Mum was home. It has been hanging

16

around for at least a week full of greasy water with a rusty Brillo pad floating in it. There isn't a dishwasher at Gramps's house, worst luck.

'You shouldn't be doing that—it's gross,' I say guiltily.

'I don't mind. I just want everything to go really well for Nell this evening. She's so excited about her party,' he says. 'Anyway, I quite like housework.'

'You like housework!' I echo with open astonishment. 'That's weird!'

He laughs and says, 'Yes, it is, isn't it? You see, my mother works full time and I take care of things at home for her. I have a little brother who needs looking after.'

'The one in the football team,' I say. I love finding out all this personal stuff about him.

'Yep, that's right. So I can cook and clean. I suppose it comes naturally to me. I'm a Libran so I like everything to be neat and looking good.'

'You'll make someone a marvellous wife one day,' I say, and then I bite at my bottom lip because it seems such a tactless, stupid thing to say.

But he laughs. 'If you like, little sis, you can do me a favour when we've finished in here. My band is playing tonight and I need to set up all the equipment and check the sound levels. Want to be my roadie?'

'Oh yes,' I say happily. 'I'd love that.'

He smiles and says: 'But first we'll wipe the worktops and mop the floor.'

'Of course,' I say enthusiastically. Doing anything with him is magic. We sweep and scrub and I am happy as Larry. I don't think Gramps would recognize his kitchen by the time we finish. Spence even does something wonderful to the Rayburn so the top is all shiny.

Nell is in a state of shock when she looks around. But she is impressed. 'There, you can do it when you want to,' she says to me.

'Now, we've worked very hard, so don't bitch,' Spence says to her. 'Just say thank you and be a nice pussy cat.'

Nell smiles at him and says sweetly, 'Thank you very much, both of you.' Then she turns to me and asks, 'Are the witches coming this evening? You'll need someone to talk to, you know.'

'The witches' is Nell's oh-so-amusing nickname for my two best friends, Hannah and Chloe. Together the three of us make up her idea of the spooks in *Macbeth*. Very clever—if you've read the play, that is.

'I don't know,' I say vaguely. Then it hits me that my phone has been strangely silent. 'I think they're coming . . .' I add lamely.

'Well, don't forget that you've promised to help me,' Spence says reassuringly and I nod shyly. As if I would forget that!

I go up to my bedroom and phone Hannah. I don't want to chat. I just want to know what time she and Clo will arrive. I am desperate to get into the bathroom before Nell hogs all the hot water so I can wash my hair and make myself look fantastic.

As soon as I hear Han's voice I know something is up.

'We're off to Leeds tonight,' she says. 'I'm really sorry. I'd come to your sister's party on my own, honestly I would. Only I can't let Chloe down. You see we're going out with Alfie and Greg—two boys from the Grammar—and Clo is really keen on Alfie.'

'It's OK. I'm helping the band set up, so I wouldn't have time to hang out with you even if you did come,' I say, trying desperately to hide the hurt in my voice.

Then I phone Chloe. I just want to say 'Good luck with Alfie,' or something nice. Something that will let her know that I'm not going to bear a grudge or sulk—even though they have dropped me right at the last moment when I'd been banking on their support.

But before I can speak she launches into an explanation: 'I'm so, so sorry about tonight,' she says, in a voice so sincere it almost melts my phone. 'Don't say anything to Hannah, will you, but I'm only doing it for her. She is crazy about this boy, Greg, and she's set me up on a double date with his best friend. There's nothing I can do!'

'You could come to the party as couples,' I say, swallowing hard.

'Well, you know, it means getting a taxi late at night from your Gramps's house and it's so expensive. And

Alfie and Greg want to go to Leeds. You will be OK, won't you?'

'Me? Oh, I'll be fine,' I mumble. I talk a bit about helping Spence and Chloe laughs as if she's guessed my secret. I hope she hasn't. I don't want to be teased about how I feel—it's too important.

'Well, that will be nice for you, won't it,' she says, as if I am a little kid. 'You won't miss us at all. And I promise we will meet up soon.'

I wash my hair with Nell's most expensive shampoo and tell myself that life is fine. Mum has promised we will stay at Gramps's house only until he has recovered from his knee op and is well enough to manage stairs and run the garden centre again. Our house in town is rented out for six months. With any luck we'll be home after Christmas and I'll be back in the swing of things.

I am unhappy they have let me down but I soon have a new panic. What am I going to wear?

I grab tops, trousers, and skirts from my wardrobe and throw them onto the bed until my room resembles the January sales. I am in despair because I have nothing special to wear. I want to look twenty instead of fifteen. What I need is an evening dress. A dress like the one I saw hanging in the tree—something sexy and snazzy that will make me look mature and even a little bit world weary.

But I've never had an evening dress like that—or any kind of dress at all apart from cotton sun-dresses and school uniform. All I've got to wear is my smart jeans and a new top. Me, Han, and Chloe always discuss what we will wear before we go out. We decided on jeans and tops for tonight because Clo's legs are sunburnt—they look like half-cooked chipolata sausages—and she said she couldn't possibly wear a skirt.

I wonder if they are wearing something totally different now for their night out in Leeds? That thought makes me feel so lonely I could cry.

Dad is back from the airport and he yells up that Mum is home so I rush downstairs. I suppose my nerves are on fire and it makes me extra sensitive. Because as soon as I see Mum, and give her a hug, I know that something is very wrong with her.

'Hi, you,' she says. 'Are you OK? Looking forward to the party?' She smiles at me, but her eyes are sad. When I press my face against her I can smell cigs and heavy Italian perfume. She never admits to cigarettes—she says other people's smoke clings to her clothes. But I know different.

'Yeah, I'm really looking forward to the party!' I say with mock enthusiasm. 'I've put Mabel in the workshop to keep her away from the cars. Have you had a good week?' I add anxiously.

Mum doesn't reply. Anyway there really isn't a chance because Nell is complaining about me. 'Honestly—it's pathetic. Hasn't she got anything better to wear than a pair of old jeans? Everyone else has made such an effort.'

'They're not old jeans,' I say indignantly. 'They are meant to look like this.'

Nell's party dress is pink with sequins and she's had her fair hair highlighted with platinum streaks. She looks totally fabulous—like a film star going to the Oscars. I feel sick with despair at the sight of her.

'It is our eighteenth,' Nell grumbles. 'Even Ed has managed to get himself into a dinner jacket and Dad is upstairs trying to make himself look smart.'

I want to ask what Spence is wearing. I hope very much that he hasn't got himself dressed up in a silly bow tie like Ed—who looks like an out-of-work conjurer.

'Shut up, Nell,' Ed says, fingering his collar as if it is choking him. 'She looks fine. And we're all pig sick of your complaints about being born into the wrong family. We all know you're a princess forced by an accident of birth to live in a hovel with a wood-cutter, a half-wit sister, and a yob of a brother, but give us a bit of a break. You've got your own way about the party—so just leave it, will you?'

'Not so much of a hovel now,' I say, trying to lighten the atmosphere because Mum hates us squabbling. I also decide to ignore the insult about the half-wit sister because I don't care what they call me—as long as Spence likes me. 'I've cleaned up the kitchen. Have you seen it?' I ask Mum, giving her another hug because she looks so unhappy.

'Yes, I popped in to see how Mrs Black is getting along with the food. It looks lovely, dear.' She drops a kiss onto my cheek but she is miles away. 'And I think your jeans look perfect. All the models at the

Milan fashion fair wore denim when they went out—dressing down is the new dressing up. Anyway, please don't argue. I'm exhausted. I'm going up to have a bath.'

'You should have come back last night. It's too much, travelling home and then my party,' Nell says, still moaning. 'I hope you won't be too tired to enjoy it. We're not having cake and champagne until midnight, you know.'

'I'll be OK,' Mum says, turning away. And if Nell wasn't so obsessed with her wonderful party she would realize that Mum is in a stress. Mum is always worn out after a week of travelling and board meetings and factory visits. Most weekends she is so tired we tiptoe around so she can catch up on sleep. But this time it's different.

'Can I make you a cup of tea, Mummy?' I ask her, because I am desperate to take away the aura of pain that surrounds her. 'Would you like to try some honey in it?'

'Thanks, poppet, that's very kind of you. I'll pass on the honey but I'd love a cup of tea. I've longed for one all week.' I really think she might cry as she says this.

Nell butts in. 'I think I shall start the evening with a gin and vermouth,' she says pertly. (We're obviously not getting in the party mood quickly enough for her.) 'Or maybe a gin and tonic with a twirl of lemon and lots of pink ice,' she continues. 'Did I tell you about the pink ice?' she asks Mum excitedly.

23

'I've put bitters in the ice tray and the cubes have come out the most marvellous colour.'

'How lovely,' Mum says, smiling. But I know she isn't really taking any of it in. She's in some other place—and it isn't making her happy.

I make Mum some tea and take it up to her room. Then I hang around on the stairs feeling a bit lost. Mrs Black has taken over the kitchen and I'm not welcome in there.

A few people start to arrive. Nell stands by the front door and greets them as if she is a duchess. Ed is left to open and close the door like the butler. Nell air-kisses everyone—playing at being a character from a costume drama on the telly.

I am just on the point of going out to the workshop to see Mabel when Spence appears and waves at me. 'There you are, little sis,' he says. 'I've been looking for you.'

I can't speak. All I can do is smile and nod. It makes me feel loads better to see that he is wearing a plain black shirt and trousers—more 'supermarket togs'. I wonder what Nell makes of it. She's so fussy about things like that.

'You didn't get made to wear a soppy dinner jacket,' I say, smiling.

He shakes his head: 'I've got better ways to spend thirty quid. Anyway, no one is going to be looking at me, are they? Everyone will be looking at you. You look absolutely gorgeous and so grown up. It's a . . .' He pauses while he searches for the right word.

'It's a transformation.' He looks so astonished. Maybe he thinks I always wear muddy shorts and have twigs in my hair.

'I really like your earrings,' he adds a bit lamely.

'Thanks, I got them in Italy,' I say. And I blush because he is glancing at me as if he can't quite believe I am real.

We rope Ed into helping with the gear. The three of us go out to Spence's van. It's an old post office one with the lettering painted over. He and Ed carry the heavy stuff into the marquee. Then I help Spence put the drum kit together and plug things in. He shows me how the mixing deck works and how to judge the sound levels of the mikes.

It's lovely being alone in the marquee with him and being taught how to be a roadie. I am disappointed when he says, 'There—all set up—the rest of the band will be here soon and we'll have a warm up. Thanks—you've been a real help.'

It's time for me to return to the party. There's no reason for me to hang around. But then, to my delight, Spence picks up his guitar and says, 'I wrote a song today.'

'How amazing,' I say. 'Will you sing it for me, please?'

He sits down on a chair and tunes up the guitar. Then he begins to sing.

> *My love is like the winter*
> *And yours is like the spring*

And when we get together
It's the most amazing thing.
But winter souls are lonely
And summer girls are fine
And when autumn comes along
Will you still be mine?'

I feel like shouting, 'Yes—yes, I will be!' But of course he's written the song for Nell not for me.

'It's very good . . .' I say helplessly. His voice is wonderful, not tuneful or anything, but magnetic.

He shakes his head and smiles at me. 'Well, there you are, little sis, you might be the first and last person in the world to hear it. I wrote it during my coffee break at work,' he adds lightly. As if writing songs in your coffee break is something that everyone does.

'It's very good. I think you should do more work on it,' I say rather formally, as if I'm his music teacher and he's just played me a composition for his GCSE coursework.

He smiles at me again, but his eyes are suddenly sad. 'I might just do that. Thanks for the vote of confidence. Now, best helper, would you like to sneak into the kitchen and get me a cold beer?'

'Yeah, of course I will,' I say brightly. And I avoid looking at him, just in case he should see all that I am feeling.

Chapter 4

The hallway is deserted. Everyone is in the sitting room or out in the garden. Above the hubbub I hear Nell's voice—a bit too shrill and excited. For as long as I can remember Nell has cried on her birthday over something. I hope that tonight will prove the exception. Mum looks low enough without a tantrum from Nell.

The kitchen is like a war zone. Mrs Black and Dot are marching around brandishing baguettes like robo-warriors. I sidle into the pantry and get some beer from the fridge. There's a lovely platter of chicken pieces cooling on the shelf. I steal a couple of drumsticks for Mabel, wrap them in kitchen roll, and sneak out through the back door.

Mabel hates being shut in the workshop. She can hear all the voices and noise and wants to be out where the action is. I carefully pull all the meat off the bones and feed it to her, remembering to wipe my greasy hands on the kitchen roll and not down my jeans. 'I know you love me,' I tell her. 'Don't slobber on me, there's a good girl. I'll come to see you later.'

I go out into the garden and around to the back of the marquee where the band has a stage entrance.

I am ridiculously happy because the bottles of beer give me an excuse to talk to Spence again.

I am just about to push open the flap of the tent and clamber up onto the stage when I realize that Spence and Nell are standing only inches from me. Their voices come across to me crystal clear and every word is like a pinch or a punch. Never was the saying, that eavesdroppers never hear well of themselves, more true.

Nell giggles. 'I never said she was twelve—you got it totally wrong, you gimp. She's fifteen—even though she acts like a retard most of the time.'

'She'll think I've been coming on to her,' Spence says miserably. 'She's young for her age, isn't she? I thought she was just a kid—the same age as my brother.'

Nell laughs and then there is a long silence. I can tell they are kissing. I back away, clasping the icy beer to my chest.

I had been nursing forlorn hopes that it wasn't really serious between them. But I am heartbroken. I can tell something special is going on there. Nell has never been really keen on anyone before. Because she's super-cool and very beautiful she always has loads of boys after her. At home the phone never stops ringing for her and she wore out two mobiles during sixth form. But she's completely different with Spence. It's as if all her guards are down. She can scream in front of him, kiss him, do whatever she wants. It is as if he belongs to her and she to him—and the whole world can know and she doesn't care.

But I care. I care very much. I've never met anyone like him before. Everything about him makes him totally loveable to me. Right down to his nose and his dreadful clothes. And to make it more complicated he really isn't Nell's type at all. Maybe it won't last long between them. This thought fills me with terror. If Nell blows him out I will never see him again . . .

I am so confused and unhappy, I need to hide. I can either return to Mabel or go up to my room. I decide on my room for the time being. But when I am on the second step of the stairs Dad calls out my name.

I turn and see him and Mum standing in the hallway staring up at me. They both look really anxious. I suppose they are worried that Gramps's house will get trashed, even though Ed and Nell have taken up all the carpets and moved most of the furniture out to the workshop.

Dad reaches up and hands me a glass of Appletize and he smiles as he says, 'It's like the rush hour in here, isn't it?'

'Have any of your friends arrived yet?' Mum asks in a concerned voice. 'I told Nell you must be able to invite someone, or it isn't fair.'

'Coming later,' I lie, because she looks so worn out. 'I've been helping the band set up,' I add, gulping at my drink to give myself something to do.

29

'Maybe we should have a whip-round and pay them to stop. It's an awful racket,' Dad says, pulling a face.

'Don't be daft,' I say grinning. 'This is a CD. The band hasn't started yet. I think they'll be really good. The singer is brilliant.'

'I was told this was going to be a quiet little get-together,' Dad says ruefully. 'I've been duped again. There seem to be hundreds of people here already.'

Nell whirls up to us. 'Darling,' she says to me. 'Please could you get a couple of bottles of wine from the kitchen and circulate with them to make sure that people have a drink. We really could have done with a pair of waiters.'

'Can't people manage to get their own drinks? It's all laid out on a table in the dining room,' I say miserably. I hate the idea of pushing through crowds of people and trying to pour wine into glasses.

'Come on, love,' Dad says kindly to me. 'I'll give you a hand. You do white and I'll do red.'

'That would be a good idea, if you don't mind. You know how clumsy she is,' Nell says. She doesn't say it unkindly and it is the sort of thing my family repeat constantly about me, but for some reason, probably because my heart is already breaking, it makes my eyes fill.

Luckily no one notices because at that moment the front door bell jangles and Ed moves forward to open the door. And the hall is suddenly packed with new arrivals.

Nell is immediately swept into the crowd, hugging

people and talking. Honestly! She must have invited everyone she has known since nursery school. It's impossible to move. I stay where I am on the stairs; because of my vantage point, I notice how the front door opens by itself, although it's no more than a crack, and a latecomer sidles in.

It is a tall spiky-haired girl. She stands behind the throng of people, looking edgy. I get the feeling she would like to push through and get into the sitting room but can't manage it. She is staring around as if she is looking for someone. Our eyes meet for a fraction of a second—but I don't have time to smile. I wonder who she is.

Nell is working her way through the group; no one is allowed to pass until they have been given the once-over and a smacker.

'Oh, hello!' Nell has reached the girl by the door. The crowd shifts, people move away. I realize with a little electric shock of surprise that I know where this girl has come from. She is wearing a red, sparkly, designer evening dress, size 10. It is still a bit creased, and next to Nell's gleaming finery and immaculate blonde hair she looks a bit grubby and frayed at the edges. Her hair is midnight black and gelled. Her ears gleam with rings and studs. And I can see now that all her fingers—even her thumbs—are covered in big silver rings. I think she looks arty and exciting. I feel a little thrill of excitement run down my back. She is a gatecrasher—an alien—someone like me who doesn't really fit in here.

31

Nell turns to find me. 'One of your friends?' she calls. There is just the tiniest frown on her face.

'Hi!' I say. And I move forward with a fake smile.

'You're not from our school, are you?' Nell says to the girl. I can see Nell's sharp eyes taking in every detail: the girl's bare legs, skinny shoulders, purple nail varnish, and rather dishevelled air. Nell was head girl at school—she knows everyone—and my circle of friends is not huge.

'No,' I say. My brain is working overtime to try to find some other explanation. 'Youth theatre—that was where we met,' I add quickly.

'Well, introduce us, please,' Nell says. She is polite but very cool. Her eyes flicker at me and I can tell that me and my rather unconventional friend are taking up too much of her time.

'This is . . .' I start to say. But then I dry up. I've used up all my inventiveness and imagination. I've never been any good at lying or acting.

'Alice,' the girl says. And I am so astonished my mouth falls open.

'Alice,' she says again. 'I'm Alice.' I notice that her London accent is so strong that her name could almost be Ellis.

'This is the other Alice,' I manage to say.

'The other Alice,' the girl echoes, and we stare at each other for a moment.

'How confusing,' Nell says. 'Anyway, it's very nice to meet you, Alice. I'm glad you could come along to keep our Alice company.'

Then she turns to me and says, 'Go and get some bottles of white wine from the fridge and do the drinks now, please.' The look she gives me is like a nudge.

Before Nell can turn away and rejoin the rest of the party the gatecrasher, Alice, says quickly, 'What an absolutely gorgeous dress—you look exquisite in it.'

Nell laughs her thanks, but I can see that the compliment has hit a bull's eye. Exquisite is just the kind of word that appeals to Nell.

'Come on in,' I say to the girl.

'Let me say hello to your parents first. Then I'll help you with the drinks,' she says. Her voice is throaty and warm and her grin wide and friendly. It seems such good fun to have a secret joke—a gatecrasher at Nell's exclusive bash—what a laugh!

I lead her across the hall and say: 'Mum, Dad, this is Alice.'

'What a lovely house,' she says to Dad. 'It's in such a great location.'

'It's my father's house and business. We are just looking after things for him. He's out of action while he's waiting for an operation on his knee,' Dad explains.

'I'm up here in Yorkshire staying with my gran,' the other Alice confides to them. 'I come up every holiday but this time Gran has had to go into hospital for a few days so I'm a bit lonely.'

'Well, then it's lovely that you have come along to the party tonight,' Mum says. And she gives me an appreciative glance because she thinks I have been a kind-hearted Samaritan. 'You must come over as much as you like while your gran is in hospital,' she adds.

'Thanks, thanks, that's really kind of you. I'll do that,' the girl says. And she looks really pleased with herself. I am surprised. She's talking as if she really will take Mum up on her invitation.

'There—that will be nice for you, won't it, Alice?' Mum says, smiling kindly.

I look into my mother's gentle, care-worn face and tiredness and depression suddenly overtake me. I hardly slept last night, thanks to the love-sick collie. Then I slid down the crag on my backside and cut my knee. And after that I fell in love for the first time. I am awash with emotion like a little rowing boat caught at sea when an Atlantic storm blows up. I need to be by myself for a little while. All I really want to do is to curl up and go to sleep. Suddenly it doesn't seem such fun any more to be lumbered with this strange girl.

And as I watch Mum and Dad talking to the other Alice I remember how much they value honesty and good behaviour. I realize that I have told a really stupid lie and for no good reason. Have I done it just for a laugh? Or was it, in some moronic way, a childish attempt to get back at Nell?

I think about Spence, who wants the party to go

really well for Nell, and think how he would despise me if he knew what I had done. And I feel terrible. I want to turn the clock back and have those moments over again. I want to disown this girl and let Nell throw her out. She is some weird camper who has got wind of the party and decided to freeload. My nerves feel raw. In a sharp moment of despair I want to tell her to piss off.

Instead I find myself walking towards the kitchen with her, and her voice is low and confidential as she asks me: 'What was the name of that play we were in? I always forget it. I was doing speed at the time and it killed off my brain cells something wicked.'

I laugh to cover my embarrassment. It's such a stupid conversation. I can't believe she's saying all this.

'Go on,' she prompts me. 'What play was it?'

'I've been in two plays,' I mumble, blushing. '*Twelfth Night* and *A Midsummer Night's Dream*.'

'That's the one,' she says happily. '"Midsummer Nightmare" was what I always called it. It's all coming back to me now. What a little shop of horrors. You were dead good. I was rubbish.'

We stop outside the kitchen door. Inside I can hear Mrs Black shouting at Dot—she is having a right moan. And—on top of that—there is the noise of the party, voices and loud music. It is all mixed up inside my head like a thudding oversized headache, making it difficult for me to think.

'But . . . but . . .' I stutter. 'I made it up. I didn't meet you at the theatre.'

'Cobblers, course you met me there,' she says cheerfully. And she links her arm through mine as if we are best buddies. 'You didn't know it was me at first cos I've dyed my hair. You still look the same.' Then she adds: 'And I recognized your parents straight away. They came to see you in the play, didn't they? Your dad's called Rob, isn't he? And he's a landscape gardener and he runs his own business.'

'Yes, yes, that's right. But I didn't . . . I didn't . . . invite . . .'

'Yeah.' She squeezes my arm. 'And I lost your number. But I heard about your party and I thought you wouldn't mind me just turning up.' She tugs at my arm as if I am a naughty puppy being brought to heel. 'We had a real good time at the youth theatre, didn't we?' she adds.

I don't answer. I am so tired. I suddenly feel completely listless. And all the time I am scrolling back through my recollections of the youth theatre. Can I really remember everyone? Was it possible that she was there and I simply can't recall her? But surely I would remember someone with the same name as me. I'm not that dozy.

'Everyone calls me Ally. You didn't know I was Alice then, did you?' she says. Just as if she knows what I am thinking. It is really, really creepy.

'No . . .' I mumble. 'I didn't know you were Alice then.'

'It's great to meet up again, isn't it?' she says confidently. I nod. I don't know what else to do. And we go into the kitchen together.

Chapter 5

Mabel wakes me at dawn. Her front paws are up on the windowsill—her head under the curtains—and she is whining. There is no way I can ignore her request to go outside. I am really worried that the Weetabix has moved through her system like a slow-moving avalanche and this is a toilet emergency.

I jack-knife out of bed and dress in the first clothes I can find in the jumbled heap at the bottom of my wardrobe.

Mabel isn't meant to sleep in with me but everything was so chaotic last night that I supposed, quite rightly, that no one would notice if I sneaked her up to my room.

I waited until midnight—when everyone was standing around the twins toasting them with champagne—before I collected her from the workshop and slipped upstairs. I felt horribly lonely and Mabel is always good company. She doesn't ask questions or tell lies—she just loves you. It's magic when you are feeling low. And it did cheer me up a bit to see how pleased she was to be in my room, and how she walked around in circles on my bed before scratching the duvet into a heap and settling herself down to sleep.

I curled up next to her and listened to the noise from the party—trying to make sense of the evening. But I had been so tired I couldn't keep my eyes open. I woke at intervals during the night—emerging from sleep like a deep-sea diver. The noise from downstairs had sounded like a riot and seemed to go on all night.

As Mabel and I race down the stairs I see that the house is a real mess and really does look as if a riot has taken place. But I am anxious to get Mabel outside and, as soon as I open the back door, I forget about everything else. The sheer beauty of the morning makes me gasp. Gramps always rises at dawn. He says it's the best time of day. Now I understand why.

The top of the crag is completely shrouded in mist like a fairy-tale castle. All the fields and woods are softened by tendrils of vapour, tinted pink by the rising sun. High above us a skylark is singing a morning song. My arms are chilly in the damp air, but after all the hot days it's delicious.

Mabel and I trot across to the gate. Then I see what woke her and started her whining. Mabel doesn't have belly-ache. She heard the sound of a van and the voices of people she knows. Because walking towards me down the lane, deep in discussion, are Nell and Spence. They are meandering slowly, arms around each other, looking every inch a couple in love. Nell is still wearing her pink party dress with a man's dinner jacket over the top.

I open the gate and Mabel runs towards them

wagging her tail and barking. Spence disentangles himself from Nell and bends down to stroke Mabel.

'Hi there, kidda,' Nell says dreamily to me. 'How are you? Wasn't it a fantastic party? Spence and I watched the sun come up. Then we went into town. We found a greasy spoon that was open down by the station and had a full English. Just the thing for a hangover! Do you know, we even had fried bread?' Nell says this in an incredulous tone—as if it's something rather exotic.

'Yuck. How disgusting! I'm glad I wasn't there,' I say, which is a huge lie. I wish desperately that I had watched the sun come up and had breakfast with Spence. 'I'm just taking Mabel for a walk,' I add lamely, conscious of my grubby clothes and untidy hair.

'Do you always get up at this time, little sis?' Spence asks me, giving one of his wonderful smiles.

'Only when Mabel wakes me,' I say, trying my hardest not to keep looking at him, but failing miserably. He needs a shave. The shadow on his jaw, combined with his black clothes, makes him look quite tough. 'It's a brill day, isn't it?' I say. And, as soon as I have spoken, I realize that my schoolgirl slang makes me sound even younger and more immature than I am—I wish I could have said something sassy and streetwise.

Miserably, I turn back to Nell. 'The house is a real tip,' I say.

'Is it?' she murmurs. 'Oh well, don't worry, we'll

soon get it tidied up. Spencer is going to brew some decent coffee—the stuff at the café was filthy—then we'll get started. It'll be done by the time the parents are up.'

'Well, I don't know about that . . .' I say uncertainly. Even to my un-house-proud eyes the house looked pretty desperate.

'Now, don't be out for too long, will you? Because we will need a hand to get tidied up,' Nell says, giving me another dreamy smile. She's away with the fairies.

'I'll make you some coffee and hot toast, ready in ten,' Spence says to me. He manages to make me feel that it is really important to him that I have breakfast and am looked after. It warms me a little. And I need it. Because seeing him and Nell together in the dawn light has struck a new coldness, like a cruel Arctic wind, straight through my heart.

I try to tell myself that it will have to be enough for me that Spence likes me as a friend, or a kid sister, and is kind to me. But a voice inside my head whispers that I want more, much more than that. I know, with chilling clarity, that I want to be where Nell is: holding onto Spence's arm, having songs written for me . . . putting my arms around his neck . . . kissing him . . . and all kinds of other things that I can conjure only in my wildest imaginings.

These moments of reckoning make me mad with fear for what the following months and years might hold. If Nell and Spence are an item I will have to see them together all the time, and maybe (horror

41

of horrors) I will have to listen to Nell's accounts of their love affair.

Nell's descriptions of her life are hilarious and plentiful. She liked nothing better when she got back from school than to tell me stories about her day. Compared to her, Ed has a really dull life—nothing exciting ever seems to happen to him! But Nell is quite different. She talks about the books she reads so the characters come alive. And she could describe an argument at school, or a teacher going ape, in a way that had me doubled over with laughter. At the same time, if she falls out with her friends, or is reading a sad book (one of the Russians or an old Thomas Hardy) I get told about it in such graphic detail that every second of pain or jealousy is utterly real to me.

I know if she tells me anything—ANYTHING—about Spence—even stuff like what size his feet are or what his favourite colour is—I might start screaming. I am so desperate at the thought of them being together in front of me that I start to make wild plans about running away.

I will go to live with Grandmamma in Sienna. I can speak and read Italian. I could finish my schooling over there. I'm not likely to do well in any important GCSEs so bunking off to Italy won't make much difference. And once I have boring old education out of the way I can get a job. Uncle Luigi might be able to find me something in his clothing factory. Or I could work in a shop. Or I wouldn't mind staying at home and cooking and cleaning for Grandmamma. I see myself in a simple summer dress, making my way to the market, basket on arm, to buy bread and vegetables and then cooking soup for our lunch.

Italy beckons like a mirage in the desert. I am always happy when I'm there. Italian boys like my fair hair and dark eyes so I always get chatted up loads. They seem enthralled by the way I speak Italian with a Yorkshire accent—and when I am shy they seem to think I am flirting. It's cool.

I cheer myself with the thought that some time, in the future, when my broken heart has healed over a bit, I will meet someone of my own to love. I reason that once I am away from Spence I will surely forget him. OK, not forget. But I might be able to put him in some compartment in the back of my mind so that the whole of my heart and soul (and whatever brain I have) isn't totally obsessed with him to the exclusion of everything else.

Mabel and I go for a very long walk while I plan my escape to Italy. By the time I get back to the house over an hour has passed and it's panic-stations in the kitchen.

Nell has taken off her posh frock and is wearing cut-off jeans and a T-shirt. Her calm lovely mood from earlier in the day has evaporated like morning mist. And now a midday heat of rage, like a plague from the Bible, is raining down upon us.

'Where on earth have you been? You useless idiot!' she shrieks at me. 'I can't believe the filth and destruction that people have left. They are all meant to be my friends. And they have behaved like a crowd of savages. There are cigarettes stubbed out everywhere and broken glass all over the garden. The whole place is a shit-tip. Dad will have a fit!'

She begins to sob and her slim body shakes as if she is a puppet being attacked by a frenzied child. Nell never does anything by half measures. I feel really sorry for her. Spence just looks across at her and frowns, which is just as well, because Nell is as likely to slap as to kiss when she is this upset.

'Don't punish yourself. It's not your fault,' I say. 'Look, please don't cry,' I beg. 'I'll put Mabel in the workshop and then I'll give you a hand. We'll soon get it sorted.'

'I'll make you a fresh coffee. You can have it while you're working,' Spence says.

'For goodness' sake will you shut up about bloody coffee,' Nell spits spitefully at him, as she mops her face with a tea towel. 'It doesn't matter if it's stewed or cold or she doesn't get to drink it. She doesn't need spoiling. She's a lazy little bitch. My father will be up soon and we need to get this place gutted!'

I turn away from her quickly, tugging at Mabel's collar, anxious to leave the room. Some tender part of me shrivels and hurts when she speaks to him like that.

As I leave I hear him say, 'Don't take it out on her, Nell. She's a good kid. She's only been walking the dog. It's not her fault.'

'Whose fault is it then? Mine?' Nell shouts, and I hurry away.

When I get back to the kitchen Spence has disappeared and Nell is filling a black bin-bag with rubbish. She stops and wipes her hand wearily across her forehead.

'Where's Ed?' I ask carefully. I don't want to set her off again.

'He's passed out on the settee in the sitting room. Spence made him some coffee but he won't get up. I'm so tired and everything is so awful,' she adds piteously.

Her lower lip quivers so much I take the bin-bag out of her hand and say: 'I'll do that. You go and make Ed get up. Tell him if he doesn't shift himself I'll cook up one of Gramps's Whitby kippers and make him eat it—bones and all. Then take Mum and Dad a pot of tea and the Sunday papers and tell them to have a lie in.'

'That's a really good idea,' she says, looking at me with surprise.

Within a couple of minutes Ed staggers into the kitchen looking like a ghoul. He fills a pint glass with cold water, slugs it down, refills it and downs it again. 'I'm going to bed,' he mutters.

'You can't do that,' I say horrified. 'You know that Dad likes everything to be clean and tidy when Mum is at home so she can have a rest. We've got to get the house cleared up. Nell is having a major breakdown.'

'Don't feel well,' he says. Then he sits down at the table and rests his head in his hands. 'It's all right for Nell—she didn't drink too much.'

'Hiya,' a voice says from behind us—and a little prickle of dismay runs down my spine at the sound of cockney vowels. I spin around and face Ally—the gatecrasher.

She stands in the doorway, grinning like a cat that has just cornered a rat. The red sparkly dress has been replaced by jeans and a skimpy T-shirt. She's had her belly-button pierced four times—it looks gross! I am suddenly really pleased I've never been allowed to have mine done. Her hair is still spiked up and she's either put on loads of Goth make-up or she is still wearing the stuff from last night. I swear, if you met her anywhere near a graveyard, you'd rush off to find garlic and a wooden stake. I'd assumed I would never see her again. I thought I could forget all about her. I am very disappointed.

'Hi . . .' I say with nil enthusiasm. 'You're up early.'

'Thought you might need a hand with the clearing up—it was quite a party, wasn't it?' she says.

'Yes, it was,' I mutter.

'You're a bit of a party pooper. What happened to you? You just seemed to disappear,' she says, as she sidles into the kitchen.

'Went to bed,' I mumble. I can hardly be bothered to speak to her. I am so fed up. As if the previous night hadn't been hard enough with no Chloe and Hannah for company, I'd also had to watch her (the girl who hadn't been invited) handing out wine and talking rhyming slang to everyone and making them laugh. She'd been the life and soul of the party. It was awful.

She moves next to Ed and smiles down at his bent head. 'Hey, Eddie! You look as if you could do with a hair of the dog,' she says jokingly. 'I'll make you one of my gran's famous hangover cures, if you like.'

She takes his silence for a 'yes'.

'Can I help myself?' she says airily to me. Before I can answer, she opens a cupboard and reaches for a clean glass, and sorts through the bottles of spirits on the worktop, just as if she owns the place.

'Fridge?' she asks.

I point to the pantry, and while I clear up I watch her out of the corner of my eye. She puts raw eggs, ice-cubes, and brandy into a cocktail shaker, shakes it slowly and then pours the contents into a tall glass. It looks utterly revolting—worse than dog sick. It's just as well that Ed is slumped down on the table apparently asleep.

She positions herself behind him and says soothingly: 'Now, Eddie. I'm going to fix your acupuncture points. Just drink this down and relax.'

She is like some old witch. She pours her vile potion down his throat, puts an ice pack on his head, and then massages his neck and shoulders with her long purple-tipped fingers.

'Now, Eddie,' she croons into his ear. 'You have a

shower and then some strong coffee and you will feel fine, I promise you.'

Ed grimaces at her. I think it is meant to be a grin. 'Thanks, Ally. You're a real pal,' he says gratefully. I suppose if you look and smell as bad as him you are grateful to anyone who gets within ten yards and is sympathetic. 'I think I feel better already,' he adds, a bit uncertainly. Then he staggers off upstairs looking green.

'He'll be fine in half an hour,' she says confidently to me. She holds out her hand. 'Got another bin-bag? I'll help you with the clearing up, if you like.'

This should make me feel friendlier towards her— but it doesn't.

'OK,' I mutter. I pass her a bag and the two of us move around the house picking up litter. It takes ages.

'Ally, you absolute angel!' Nell says, when she comes to find us and discovers that we have cleared the whole house of rubbish. 'Thanks so much for coming to help. I feel so let down by my friends. No one has come back to help and everyone made such an awful mess.'

'Yeah, well I know how it is. I had the same thing at my last party,' Ally says. Her voice is low and confidential as if she and Nell are sharing a secret together. 'My mother's flat got totally trashed and her jewellery got stolen. She had this really priceless engagement ring and it got nicked. We had to call the police in. I was gutted.'

'Really, how terrible!' Nell says in an awestruck

tone. She seems to have momentarily forgotten her own troubles and be fixated by this account of Ally's misfortunes. 'Was it taken by someone you knew? Or was it a gatecrasher? Did your mother ever get her ring back?'

I turn away quickly. My face feels hot and my head is throbbing. I can't bear to hear any more. The word gatecrasher is like a pain sawing away at my temples. I go up to the bathroom, have a shower, and then I go into my bedroom and lock the door.

I am utterly fed up with picking up cig ends and paper cups and bits of half-eaten food. As far as I can see, there is absolutely no chance of getting the house cleaned before Mum and Dad get up. And, to add to my complete misery, I haven't had any breakfast—not even a cup of tea.

I dress slowly in clean clothes. My head is full of muddled images from the day before: the crag and the jumping stones, the campsite, the sparkly red dress hanging on a branch, and finally Ally arriving at the party.

Then I begin to trawl further back in time to when I was in the youth theatre: the Victorian red-brick theatre in town and the studio where we rehearsed; the cramped dressing rooms shared between six and the dark wings, musty with the smell of old clothes; the boredom of rehearsals and the terror of perform-ance. And then there were the faces, the friends I'd made, and the people I had known. Ally isn't among them.

Under my bed, in shoe boxes, is my attempt at a filing system. I scrabble through loads of junk: school-work, exercise books, paintings, and postcards before I finally find a photo album and some loose photos.

I locate what I want—a large group photo still in a clear envelope. It shows the cast of *A Midsummer Night's Dream* in costume. I scan the faces but it is impossible to put names to them all—or even to be sure who it is under all the masks and make-up. I throw it down, disappointed. I want to know if she really had been there. But the official photo is no help at all.

Tucked underneath it is a sneaked photo of me in my fairy costume pulling a face—I look a complete freak. The boy who took the picture is called Sam. He was my partner in the dances and when the show finished he gave me a toy white rabbit as a present. This was because he was always teasing me about being called Alice and telling me not to talk to any cats or fall down any rabbit holes.

Sam also had a digital camera and was always taking pictures. His dad runs a photographic studio in town. I scrabble around until I find a notebook full of phone numbers. Sam and I were really good friends. And we said we would keep in touch—we'd been as close and connected as a pair of baby birds while we were rehearsing and performing. But once we were back at our own schools it never seemed to happen.

I am really shy about phoning people out of the

blue—I've never had the nerve to ring him. But I am so fired up about Ally that without a second thought I reach for my mobile and tap in his number. It is only when I hear his sleepy voice answering that I remember it is Sunday morning and still really early.

His voice is warm and husky, deeper than I remember it. I suddenly recall his face: the sharp lines of his cheekbones, his brown-blond hair that falls over his eyes, and his infectious laugh. I remember how he would say my lines for me in a high squeaky voice when I forgot them—and how he spent ages teaching me the steps to our dances. I am alone in my room but my face heats to a dreadful blush and I begin to stammer. I am suddenly filled with a cold terror that, despite all the camaraderie and the white rabbit, he might have forgotten me entirely.

By some miracle he works out it is me and not some random nuisance caller. 'Alice! Hi! It's great to hear from you. How's life in Wonderland?' He is disarmingly pleased to talk to me—even though I have obviously woken him up—and it is such a relief that once again I don't know what to say.

I mumble on for a while. He seems puzzled by my half-finished sentences. Eventually he takes control and says, 'Let me get this straight. You want to see pictures of the cast from *The Dream*?'

'Yes, that's right,' I say with relief.

'OK, that's cool,' he says kindly. 'Any particular reason?'

'Yes, but I can't explain over the phone,' I say uncertainly.

'It's OK. I'll dig out my pics—I've got them stashed somewhere. Shall we meet up in town later?'

'I'll have to see when I can get a lift. We're staying out at my gramps's garden centre at Ramsgarth and there aren't any buses on a Sunday.'

'I'll cycle out to you, if you like,' he says.

'It's a long way . . .'

He laughs. 'Some time after lunch?' he suggests.

I start to try to give him directions but after teaching me to dance he knows better than anyone that I muddle up left and right. So he laughs again and says he'd better look at a map or he might end up in Scarborough. But he says it in a jokey way.

'See you later, Alice; it's great to hear from you again,' he says. And he sounds as if he really means it. And I suddenly feel loads more cheerful.

Chapter 6

I feel quite light-headed with relief after I have spoken to Sam. During the youth theatre he was really competent and well organized—not dizzy and forgetful like me. If anyone can sort out the puzzle of Ally, and who she really is, it will be him. I am sick of thinking about her. I just want to know if she really was at the theatre with us and then forget all about her.

The kitchen is empty. I fix myself some cornflakes and juice and then start washing up. When I've finished I clean the worktops and the cooker and mop the floor—just like Spence did last night. After all that work I'm starving again. And I expect everyone else is too. So I make a huge pile of bacon sandwiches and a big bowl of salad and set the table. I do it all to show off to Spence. I long for his admiration on any terms.

I shout at the back door that lunch is ready and one by one people drift into the kitchen. I have been hoping that Ally would have disappeared by now. But she comes into the kitchen with Ed—yakking away to him as if he's her best friend. I can't believe that she's still hanging around and that someone—probably Ed, the twit—has invited her to stay for lunch.

'What a feast. Thank you very much, Alice, love,' Dad says, smiling at me. He's always grateful if we help with the cooking because he does all the housekeeping when Mum is away.

'We'll give thanks for our food,' he adds quietly. It's a tradition in our family that we say grace. Spence is waiting like the rest of us. But while Dad is speaking Ally grabs a sandwich and moves it towards her mouth. I avert my eyes for a moment.

'Oh hell,' she mutters.

Dad ignores this: 'We ask your blessing, Lord, and thank you for the precious gift of this food. Amen.'

To cover her embarrassment everyone but me makes a great noise and rushes about handing out the sandwiches and passing the salad dressing. I simply watch her—conscious of my pleasure at her discomfort. It serves her right for pushing herself in and pretending she's one of the family. My meanness is gratified. She is staring down at the sandwich on her plate and her hands are balled into fists. She is really tense, blinking too fast . . . *She looks as if she is going to cry.*

Guiltily, I look away and chew my sandwich slowly. When I glance back, she is staring at Dad with the strangest look on her face. I would have thought she'd be annoyed with him. We could have missed grace for once—it is only sandwiches after all. But the expression on her face isn't irritation. I can't for the life of me describe what it is. She's gazing at him as if he is an Old Testament prophet who has just dropped out of heaven and landed in our kitchen.

To my horror—just as we are finishing our sand-wiches—Mum starts to ask me what Ally and I are doing after lunch, as if we are an inseparable twosome like Tweedledum and Tweedledee. 'You two girls have done enough cleaning,' Mum says kindly. 'Why don't you take Mabel for a walk?'

I am so relieved I phoned Sam or I might have got lumbered with Ally for the rest of the day.

'I'm busy this afternoon,' I mumble, through a mouthful of crust. 'Sam is coming over.' I swallow hastily. 'And I've got to get on with my course-work as well.' I am clutching at straws: gabbling to fill the space in the conversation and the unnerving feeling that everyone's eyes are on me.

'Oh dear, Alice, are you still struggling with your course-work?' Mum asks anxiously. 'I thought you said it was nearly finished. Did you get the computer fixed?'

'It's still away . . . problems with the hard drive. I'm writing it out by hand,' I say. The truth is that doing my holiday work has been like wading through treacle—but I don't want Mum to know that. 'Anyway, Ally's busy this afternoon. She's got to go to see her gran in hospital, haven't you?' I say. And I stare at her defiantly—daring her to contradict me.

'Yeah, yeah, that's right. I have,' she says. And she shoots a curious sideways glance at me before turning her attention back to my parents. 'Gran loves me visiting her. She says I brighten up her whole world. Trouble is I can't stay long because she gets so tired.'

'That must be very hard on you,' my mother says sympathetically.

'Would you like a lift to the hospital,' Dad asks kindly. 'No buses today.'

'I've got my car with me,' Ally says, somewhat regretfully. I get the feeling she's loving being the centre of attention.

'And what a car it is,' Ed says with a grin. 'Ally took me for a spin up to the main road and back and we had the roof down.'

'A convertible?' Nell asks longingly.

Ed laughs. 'Eat your heart out, Nell. It's a real swank mobile. It's a metallic-pink Beetle convertible—with personalized number plates. Ally got it for her nineteenth birthday,' he adds proudly, as if he'd given it to her himself. Honestly, boys make me sick sometimes.

'Really?' Nell says, and she gazes at Ally with frank, and not totally flattering, astonishment.

'But I thought you were the same age as our little Alice,' Mum says, looking puzzled. 'I didn't realize you are older than the twins.'

'I'm nearly twenty,' Ally says.

Nell says enviously, 'You are really lucky to have a car like that.'

Nell and Ed have passed their tests and they share Gramps's old Metro between them. Nell would love a pink trendy car with her own special number plate. It's just the image she craves. Whereas I would never have anything like that—I'd be too embarrassed. I'd feel as if I was begging people to look at me.

'My so-called-father gave it to me,' Ally says, staring at Nell with dark unblinking eyes. 'He comes over from America only a couple of times a year so he tries to spoil me rotten when he does—just to make up for the fact that he's a crap dad.'

She turns away from Nell and gives Dad a long look. Then she adds in an intense voice, 'It's all guilt money. And I'd swap the car, and all the other stuff he lavishes on me, to have a proper dad—someone who was around all the time and was really interested in me.'

This is terrible. She sounds like someone on a daytime confessional chat-show. Nell breaks in quickly. 'Spencer's father lives in America too. Where is it exactly that he lives, Spence?'

Spence steps in obligingly: 'He lives in Washington DC. He's remarried now and has two baby daughters—Poppy and Daisy. They're really sweet.'

'And he has an interesting job, doesn't he?' Nell prompts.

'Yes, he works for the Federal Government—his job is very hush hush. He's also a baseball coach. He's a pretty cool guy.' Spence smiles and I hold my breath. I love to hear him talking about his family and long to hear more. But annoyingly Ally cuts in.

'My father lives in Florida. And he works for NASA,' she says. 'He has a really top secret post to do with space weapons so I'm not really supposed to talk about him.'

She looks around the table and frowns at us

all—as if she is weighing up in her mind if we can be trusted. Then her voice drops, as if she fears she might be overheard: 'When he comes to Europe he has the maximum national security code Alpha/One and a bodyguard. It's pretty strange going out for lunch with him, I can tell you.'

'How extraordinary—it's like something out of a film!' Nell says. Everyone looks enthralled and impressed and I feel irrationally irritated. It sounds like a load of baloney to me.

'I've finished. Shall I make some tea?' I ask. 'Sam will be here soon,' I add.

'This Sam who is coming over this afternoon—is it a boy Sam or a girl Sam?' Nell asks.

'Boy Sam,' I mumble, as I switch on the kettle. I was going to add, *It's someone I know from the youth theatre,'* but the words stick in my throat.

'A boy Sam! A boyfriend! Why didn't you ask him to come along last night? Then you wouldn't have been such a wallflower,' Nell says, with a little laugh.

Dad gives Nell a warning glance, Spence looks up at me with a sympathetic smile, and I know immediately that 'wallflower' is no-way a compliment.

My last mouthful of sandwich seems to have got lodged somewhere between my mouth and my stomach. I feel totally stressed—and it's not just Nell's bitching. I don't trust Ally and I don't believe anything she says. I feel contaminated by her presence and her pretend friendship. I want her to go away. How I felt when I found the red dress on the crag has come back to haunt me. I feel all chewed up inside, frightened and confused, as if something evil is waiting to jump out on me.

I refuse to say another word and Mum obviously feels that I am being rude. She fusses over Ally when she leaves and tells her to come again soon, and how lovely it has been to see her, and we all have to go outside to wave her off.

'Why haven't you ever invited Ally around before? She's great, isn't she?' Ed says to me, staring regretfully at the sparkly pink Beetle as it drives away. 'Shame she had to go. I was hoping for another ride in her car.' He gives me a slightly shocked sideways glance—as if he can't believe I've got such a cool friend, with such a cool car. Yuck!

'It was so good of her to come back and help with the clearing up. She's a star,' Nell says.

'She certainly is,' Ed agrees. 'And she knows how to cure a hangover. No one has ever found my acupuncture points before,' he adds musingly.

'The best way to cure a hangover is not to drink too much in the first place,' I say grimly.

It's sickening the way they are going on. They both seem to love Ally and believe every word she says. No one bothers to reply to me so I add: 'Anyway—I'm glad she's gone. And I hope I never ever see her again.'

They both stare at me with disbelief. They obviously think I'm crackers. Maybe I am. I don't understand why I dislike Ally so much. I just have this gut reaction that she's not what she seems. I avoid their eyes and say lamely, 'I'm going to let Mabel out now as there's no sign of that wretched collie.'

'Do you know something, Alice,' Nell says, 'your social skills are abysmal. It's a miracle that you have nice friends like Ally if you are always so off-hand with them.' Her tone of voice implies that she is telling me this for my benefit and I should be deeply grateful.

'And,' Nell continues bossily, 'I don't know why on earth you invited her to my party if you don't like her. But we're very pleased that you did. She's a real laugh.' I am being totally put in my place.

Suddenly I am sick of the whole deception, and I say loudly, 'If you want to know the truth, I didn't invite her to your party. I don't remember her at all from the youth theatre. And I don't know who the hell she is!' I take a deep breath to try to stop my chin from trembling. I am on the verge of getting upset.

To add to my pain, Ed, Nell, and Spence all burst out laughing, as if I've just told some hilarious joke.

'Oh dear me, it's just as well that she remembers you, isn't it?' Nell says gaily.

'Poor old kidda, you've got a memory like a sieve, haven't you?' Ed adds.

And they all laugh again—even Spence. And I turn away, feeling hurt and confused, because I don't see what is so bloody funny.

I am so upset I have to go and hug Mabel until I feel better. Then I hang around outside, waiting for

Sam to arrive. I hardly recognize him when he whirls into the yard on a mountain bike. He's got really tall and his hair is short and spiky, not silky and flopping in his eyes like it used to be. He gets off his bike and we stand and stare at each other for what seems like ages.

'It's really good to see you,' I say politely.

'Yeah,' he says. He swings his rucksack and looks away as he adds: 'It's great to see you too. I brought those pics you want.'

'OK, thanks,' I say. 'Would you like a cold drink?' I add, remembering Nell's rude comment about my social skills.

'Yes . . . thanks,' he says.

We go into the kitchen. Everyone has disappeared. I can hear the sound of the Hoover in the sitting room. The big clean-up goes on. Mum and Dad will be working until midnight. The kitchen is OK but the rest of the house is trashed.

I get us some juice from the fridge and we sit down at the table. For a while we talk about school, GCSEs, and who we hang out with.

Then he says, 'You were upset when you phoned, I could tell. Why do you want to see pictures of the youth theatre?'

I don't reply immediately. I had forgotten how direct he is. His blue eyes are gazing at me as if he can see right inside my head. It is a year since we were in *The Dream* together. He has changed so much that he seems like a stranger. Just for a moment I toy with the idea of laughing the whole thing off, not telling him anything, pretending it never happened. Now I have to actually talk about it, it seems completely crazy—like a nightmare.

'Come on, Alice, spit it out. Or has the big Cheshire Cat got your tongue again?' He grins at me. And suddenly, behind the manly grown-up exterior, I see the boy I knew. Despite the thinner face, stubble, and macho hair, I recognize the Sam I worked with in drama improvisations. I recall how he patiently taught me to dance, holding me in his arms until we were both hot and laughing. He also covered up for me endlessly when I forgot my lines, sparing me many humiliations. He was the best friend ever.

I am not a natural for the stage. Mum insisted I joined the youth theatre 'to build my confidence'. In contrast, Sam loves singing, dancing, and acting and hopes to go to drama school. But he never complained about being partnered with a loser like me. In fact he seemed to positively relish his role as my coach. I'd had a good time during *The Dream* largely because of him. Remembering it all makes me know I can trust him. I begin to talk.

'This girl arrived here. The other Alice . . .'

It takes me ages to explain. Sam listens patiently—every so often he asks me a question as if he is a detective. We could be filmed and used as a script for a 'whodunit'. Only we don't have a crime, a body, or anything concrete to go on. All we have is a weird girl from London, a campsite up on the crag, a lie that seems to have an existence of its own, and my uncomfortable feelings.

We spend ages going through his pictures. I even find a magnifying glass so we can study them close up. But the photos show us nothing. Although they do jog our memories! We had been in the fun group, but there had been some people who hadn't joined in very much. A sulky girl we nicknamed Gladys— neither of us could remember her real name. There had been a snobby pair called Tilda and Serena who obviously thought that everyone from a state school was common. There were also a couple of geeky boys who never spoke to anyone but each other. We discussed the possibility that Ally was there too and we didn't even notice her. We'd had such a good time—too good a time to bother with boring people.

Finally we put the pictures away and sit back in our chairs and look at each other.

'She's older than us. She said she was nearly twenty.'

'Do you think she is still using the campsite? And why would she be camping if she's got loads of money? And how does that fit in with looking after her gran?'

I shake my head. It's all starting to sound barmy. I am worried Sam will think I'm making it up.

'Let's go up to the crag and those jumping stones and see if her tent is still there,' Sam says decisively.

'Go up to the crag . . .' I echo nervously.

'Yeah. Then we'll know if she's still hanging around. I really want to meet her.'

'I've always hated the crag and the woods,' I say miserably, as I put Mabel on her lead. 'And when I first saw Ally's red dress hanging in a tree I thought it was a body and I was really scared,' I confess. I am shamefaced, certain he will laugh at me.

'Hey, there's nothing to be frightened of now. You'll be with me,' Sam says reassuringly, giving me a sympathetic look. 'Come on, Alice, let's get going.' He holds his hand out to me. 'I promise I'll take care of you.'

'OK,' I say, and I let him take my hand and keep hold of it as we leave the house and set off for the woods. If Nell or Ed see us holding hands they'll think he's my boyfriend and tease me like mad, but I don't mind. It's lovely to be close to him—really comforting. It's just what I need.

Chapter 7

It's impossible to keep Mabel on her lead in the dark wood. She pulls so much that Sam can't hold her. 'Let her off—I think she'll be OK,' I say breathlessly.

I am astonished that I managed to get through the wood and up to the top so quickly when I was on my own—because it takes Sam and me ages to fight our way through the dense trees and undergrowth.

Mabel is delirious with happiness to be back in the dark wood. She spends the whole time snuffling about, digging frantically in the leaf mould, and then eating what she finds.

'What is it she's gobbling down?' Sam asks. 'She's going at it as if it's chocolate.'

'Worms? Roots? Fungi? Mud? There are lots of possibilities and all of them disgusting. Best not to ask,' I say, and he laughs.

'Wow, it's amazing up here—it's like being on top of the world,' he yells, as we reach the highest point of the crag. The whole of the valley and the river are spread out for us to view as if we are birds. Down below us the farm, the tractor, and the animals in the fields all look like toys from a child's farmyard set. And distance softens the sun-bleached fields to a chalk-yellow and pastel-green patchwork.

'I don't like heights,' I say nervously, looking away quickly. 'When I came here before I went straight over the top. But there is a path over there.'

Sam takes hold of my hand again and squeezes it comfortingly. 'For someone who doesn't like heights you did pretty well to go straight down.'

'I was worried about Mabel,' I explain. 'I didn't know if the collie was lurking around. Gramps would be mega-upset if Mabel got pregnant while I'm in charge of her. I don't want the reputation of someone who is too thick to look after a bitch on heat, do I?'

No,' he says, smiling. He peers over the side of the crag. 'It's a bit of a scramble but it isn't too steep. There are lots of branches and things to grab. Let's climb down. Come on, Alice, do it! Then you'll never be frightened of it ever again.'

I pull a face and he adds, 'Honest. It's not difficult. I'll guide you down. Come on.'

Sam shows me how to face the rocks and go down as if I am climbing a ladder. It didn't occur to me last time to try it that way—I just hurled myself over. He stays close to me, with a reassuring arm around my waist, and shows me how to find hand- and footholds. It seems so easy when he's helping me; I'm not scared at all.

It's only when we get to the jumping stones that my heart starts to thud and my throat tightens. The memory of the red dress fluttering like a flag signalling danger is still stuck inside my head. I can't seem to get rid of it.

'There's no one here and nothing to see,' Sam says in a disappointed voice. But I am relieved that Ally's not here. I never want to see her again.

'The dress was hanging on the oak tree,' I whisper. 'And the tent was under there.' I point with a finger that isn't quite steady. I feel as nervous as a kitten stranded in a tree.

Mabel is sweeping the area with her nose to the ground like a mine detector. But Sam's right—there's nothing here. Nothing to support my story . . . it's as if I dreamt the whole thing.

'I really did see it all: the red dress, the tent, the litter,' I say, a bit uncertainly.

'Look, there're marks where the tent has been. And here's some food . . . Or rather there was some food—a half-eaten sandwich—but Mabel got it,' Sam says excitedly. 'She was here! I wonder where she parked her car and why she camped here? There must have been a reason for it.' Sam's eyes are narrow with concentration. I like the way he talks as if we are detectives on the telly.

He walks right to the edge of the jumping stones and then calls excitedly to me: 'Alice, get a look at this!'

'I don't do edges,' I say weakly. 'It's a sheer drop and I have vertigo and falling-down-cliffs-phobia.'

'Give over,' he says. He is laughing as he comes back to me. 'I'll hold on to you. I want you to see.

Come on, Alice . . .' He grabs me around the waist and pulls me over to the ledge. I am terrified. I cling on to him like a baby koala that has found the last gum tree in the world and is not going to let go.

'Look, Alice,' he says, and his voice is urgent and excited. 'From here you can see right down to your back door, the greenhouses, and the drive. It's like looking in on the *Big Brother* house. She's been sitting here and spying on you all.'

'How do you know that?' I ask weakly. I don't like to think of her doing that. I want him to be wrong.

'Look!' he says. He points down to the edge of the stone. There is a natural hollow the size of a small bowl. *It is full of cigarette stubs.* 'She sat up here, smoking and watching you all. I'm sure of it!'

I am astonished and I grip him so tightly it would be embarrassing in normal circumstances. But I am too nervous and upset to care. 'Why would she want to look at us? It's just too weird. We're not exactly fascinating, are we? I mean, Nell has a pretty interesting life but Ed is the original Mr Boring. Mum is away most of the time and all Dad does is work, shop, cook, and clean. And as for me . . . well, my life makes *Big Brother* look like an epic adventure.'

He moves me back from the ledge. We are still clasping each other as if it is impossible to let go, and we fall in a tumble of arms and legs onto the grass. 'Well, you have interesting friends,' he says with a grin. Then he adds: 'And don't put yourself down. I like you just the way you are.'

Then he puts his arms around me again and pulls me into a proper hug. I am aware of our damp T-shirts and the hot smell of his skin. We are wrapped up close like we used to be when we danced together. But this time it's different—there is a buzz, like electricity, between us. It's lovely to be cuddled by him. I give in to a moment of extreme pleasure and comfort.

'Alice,' he says. His tone is suddenly serious. I have a premonition of what is coming next. I have dreamed of a time when someone liked me enough to ask me out properly but now I am in turmoil.

'Alice,' he starts again, 'will you be my girlfriend? I mean, not just a friend. More than a friend . . . A couple . . . You know what I mean, don't you?'

'Yes.'

'Well?'

'I'm going away to Italy soon for a three-week holiday—' I blurt out.

'OK. That's cool. I am thinking of a long-term commitment so I guess I can wait three weeks.' He is teasing me and I blush. His face is pressed against mine and I wonder if he can feel the heat.

His voice is relaxed and happy as he says, 'I was so chuffed you called me. I thought you were really special when we were in *The Dream* together. I couldn't do anything about it then because I was going out with a girl from school, but that's all over now.'

'I . . .' I can't get any words out because I don't

know what to say. His mouth is nuzzling my cheek and I know he is going to kiss me. For a moment I long to put my arms around his neck and kiss him first. I think about saying 'YES' to him and how cool and wonderful it would be to have a boyfriend like him. Someone good-looking and kind and funny— someone who makes me laugh and (miracle) laughs at my jokes too. Someone who thinks I am special and important, even though he has seen me at my most vulnerable—falling over my feet in dances and forgetting my lines in rehearsal. I am so grateful to him—and so upset—that I want to cry.

I think about phoning Hannah and Chloe when I get home, telling them they aren't the only ones to have boyfriends, that I too am part of a couple. I think about introducing them to Sam and seeing the surprise in their eyes that someone like him wants to go out with someone like me.

If only he had asked me before the party it could all have been so different. If I had been committed to him I would never have let myself fall in love with Spence. I would have fought it—defeated it— hidden it away. But it is way too late for any of that. And—just for a moment—I hate myself because Sam is so lovely—and yet my treacherous heart is wishing it was Spence hugging me. I pull away quickly.

'I'm sorry. It isn't just going away to Italy. There is someone . . .' I can see by the shocked look on his face that I misled him earlier. We talked about school and our friends and we both signalled pretty clearly that we were unattached.

'I'm not going out with anyone—nothing like that,' I say lamely. I am conscious that I am making a real mess of the whole business. I wouldn't blame him if he never wanted to talk to me again after this. 'It's just there's someone I think a lot about—who I have feelings for. And I don't think it would be fair—I mean . . .'

'Does this person have feelings for you?' he asks me. He is still holding me but there is a coolness, a restraint, in him. I guess I have hurt him—am still hurting him.

'No,' I say sadly. 'Not like that. I mean, I think he likes me but that's all.'

'It's pretty hard having those sorts of feelings for someone who doesn't care,' Sam says gently. 'It's a lonely place to be. I know. I went on holiday to Turkey with a friend of mine who has family over there. I met this girl—a friend of his cousins—and she got under my skin like an illness. I couldn't sleep or eat or stop myself thinking about her. It was madness. I got to feeling that I couldn't come home and leave her. And all the time she was teasing and flirting with me and my friend. And when I wanted to talk to her he had to speak for me because my Turkish is appalling. And it was quite difficult to say what I wanted to say like that. Then, during the last few days of the holiday, she made it very clear that she had fallen for him. They got it together like Romeo and Juliet and I had to sit and watch.'

'Oh Sam,' I say in a sad whisper. 'That's awful . . .'

'I can remember getting on the plane and sitting next to him and feeling as if the world had ended. I felt as if I'd lost everything. After that I made a vow I would be more careful who I fell in love with.' He laughs then, and there is just an edge of bitterness to the sound. 'Who is he?' he asks suddenly, and his voice is tense.

I feel I owe it to him to tell the truth. Also, my feelings for Spence are like a weight around my soul, I long to unburden myself to someone.

But, before I can reply, he puts his hand gently against my mouth to stop me from speaking. 'Sorry, Alice. I shouldn't have asked that. Don't tell me. It isn't any of my business.'

He moves right away from me then. And I feel bereft and lost and despite the warmth of the day a shiver runs down me.

I put my hand on his arm and whisper urgently. 'I want to tell you. I need to tell someone. It's Nell's new boyfriend, Spence. And he's not her type at all and I don't know what is worse: thinking about them being together all the time or thinking about them finishing and maybe never seeing him again. You're right—it is like madness. I wish I didn't feel it, but I do.'

I begin to cry then and once I start I can't stop. Sam folds me up in his arms as if I am a baby and holds me tight.

'I'd like . . . I want . . . You are . . .' I am blubbing so much I can't get out what I want to say. Typically Sam works it all out anyway.

'When you get back from Italy we'll talk again. We're friends whatever happens. Aren't we?' he says kindly. He stands up. 'Come on,' he says, and he reaches out his hand to me. I mop my face with a sodden tissue and let him pull me to my feet.

And then, as if to prove to me what a fool I am (as if I need reminding) he kisses me gently, full on the lips. It is indescribably gorgeous. I don't kiss him back. I just stand like a dummy—as if I've been hit over the head with a sandbag rather than swept away by passion. The kiss ends. He pulls away and avoids my eyes. It is then that the enormity of what I have done really catches up with me and I stumble down the hill after him dazed with misery.

Hannah and Chloe phone to tell me about their rave night in Leeds. I lie through my teeth and say the party was fantastic and I'd had a great time. I can't bring myself to tell them about Ally, how she had been hiding up on the crag and watching us all, and how she gatecrashed the party. All my uncomfortable feelings about her can't be translated into words. Not ones I can say to them anyway.

Sam is another topic I can't talk to them about. How do I start to explain that I have been asked out by someone I really, really like but I said 'No'? Because if I told them about Sam I'd have to explain

73

about Spence—but I am totally confused about him so what chance do I have of making them understand? The way they talk about Greg and Alfie—giggling and making jokes—is so different to how I feel about him.

I hate myself for lying to them. It seems like the end of our friendship. Because there seems no logic in having best mates I can't confide in and tell the truth to.

They say we must all meet up. I say I have too much packing to do. They talk about their holiday and tell me how lucky I am to be going to Italy.

I am so involved with my own problems and confusions—one minute planning a new life away from Spence, the next fearful and upset at the thought of not seeing him for three weeks—that it escapes my notice that Mum hasn't got packed up and ready to leave.

She comes into my bedroom to see me. I have made an excuse about schoolwork to get away from everyone and I am lying on my bed listlessly looking through my history course-work folder.

'Is it interesting?' Mum asks.

'It's the role of women during the First World War,' I say in answer.

'Are you enjoying it?'

'Mum, you don't enjoy history. You just do it.'

'You can do well in subjects only if you enjoy them. You must try to find pleasure in studying, like Nell does,' she says gently.

This seems such a tall order. Isn't it enough that I do the work?

'It's easy for Nell,' I say a bit sulkily.

'I know it is.'

She looks so unhappy that I force a smile and say, 'I will try.'

She sits down on the edge of my bed. 'Alice, I'm afraid I have some difficult news.'

'It isn't Gramps, is it?' I cry out in panic.

'No! Gramps is fine. I know he's miserable being with Auntie Jess. She's so house-proud and he misses Mabel. But once he's had his operation he'll be back to his old self. No, it's about my job.'

'Your job?' I say, startled. Mum has worked with her extended family in Italy since I started school. She flits between London and Milan, and it isn't just a job, it's a way of life. We holiday in Italy with the family and all the time they talk shop—materials, fabrics, fashions, and factories. They make ready-to-wear clothes for women. It's a world away from Dad's gardening business. Mum's work has been so much a part of my life that I have never given it a second thought. It's just something that has always been there—like the sun and the moon.

'What's happening with your job?' I say. 'You are still going to be able to come home at the weekends, aren't you?' I add anxiously. Mum works such long hours—if she works any harder we will never see her.

Mum nods. I can see tears glistening in her eyes.

'Weekends, weekdays, I shall be here. I have been made redundant. I am no longer working. I have been given a month's salary in lieu of notice. Luigi suggested I clear my desk and come home. He said it would save tears and I think he was right. He reminded me that I have been saying for years that I want to spend more time with my family and now I have the chance.'

'But why? Why have they done it?'

'A big recession in the market—several important contracts lost. The London office is to close.' Mum can hardly get the words out she is so close to tears.

I put my arms around her and hold her tight. 'I'm sorry . . .' I say. I would like to argue: to say that the family can't do this to her and that it isn't fair, not after all the years she has worked so hard for them. But I don't think it would make it any easier for her. She must know all that.

'It will be lovely to have you at home,' I say.

'Yes, it will be lovely to be at home,' she says. 'But it does mean that money will be tight until I get another job. And I'm afraid we won't be going to Italy this year. I know how much you love going there and spending time with the family. I do feel for you—but I simply can't face it.'

'It's OK,' I say bravely. 'I don't mind not going. I have been a bit worried about leaving Mabel anyway,' I add, and that bit at least is true. 'I know Dad said he would look after her and everything, but she is a lot of work and he's always so busy. I don't mind staying here for the summer, honestly. I can help Gary in the shop. And when the computer comes back I can spend lots of time typing up my history course-work.'

'Yes,' Mum says a bit absentmindedly. I get the feeling that my arrangements for the summer are the least of her problems. 'Nell and Ed will have to get jobs and save some money for university. It was going to be a struggle even with my income. It's going to be very hard now.'

'We'll manage. Don't worry,' I say, and I give her another hug.

Mum kisses me and murmurs, *'Ti voglio bene e tu sei la mia bimba speciale'*—she loves me and I am her special baby.

She leaves, but I stay lying on my bed staring at the ceiling. I am too upset to cry. For a while I make myself concentrate on the cracks in the plaster that look like a river with tributaries, and the yellowing damp patch over the window that is roughly the shape of an elephant—anything to take my mind off what has happened.

Since finding the red dress at the crag everything seems to have gone crazy. Ally is like a bad fairy who arrived at the party and cast an evil spell over the world. Everything in my life is fracturing and changing and going wrong, wrong, wrong: Spence, Sam, Mum, and now my holiday and chance to see Grandmamma. My world and my heart are spinning out of control.

Chapter 8

Early on Monday morning I wake to the sound of an argument in the kitchen. I pull the sheet over my head but it does nothing to block out the raised voices from down below.

I screw up my eyes and wish myself back to sleep, but it doesn't work. Reluctantly, I get up and go downstairs. Ed and Nell are standing around the kitchen table having a slanging match. Dad is standing in resigned silence listening to them.

'Don't be such a frigging snob,' Ed rages at Nell. 'You can't afford to be fussy. Have you any idea how much it costs to be a student? And especially to live in London.'

'And when did you last visit our capital city?' Nell snaps. 'Don't talk down to me. I know just as much as you do. I just want to wait and get a job I enjoy rather than rushing off to that awful supermarket and grabbing the first thing that's on offer. I might get put on the meat counter or something really gross.' Nell does one of her wonderful theatrical shudders at the thought. She's always been an emotional, if not a practical, vegetarian.

'Fat lot of frigging use you'll be on the meat counter, or any other counter come to that . . .' Ed starts again.

'Please!' Dad interjects at last. 'Please can we discuss this rationally and sensibly without swearing and abuse? I didn't get you both up early to row. And please keep the volume down—I really don't want your mother woken up.'

'Well, you've woken me up. What's going on?' I ask sleepily. 'It's so early,' I complain, as I look at the clock on the wall. Nell and Ed are dressed and ready to go out which is utterly amazing at this time of the morning.

Neither of them is concerned about me. They don't even look in my direction. They simply carry on arguing.

'I thought you would have jumped at the chance of a job at the supermarket. Spence has worked there for years and he loves it,' Ed says to Nell. 'He says it's a great firm and that we can put him down as a reference on our forms.'

'Shut up!' Nell says furiously, as if she resents Ed even mentioning Spence's name, just as though he's her property and Ed is trespassing. 'I don't want to work there. It's full of fat people buying junk food, screaming kids, and yobs shoplifting. And the staff have to wear a vile uniform. It's made of synthetic fibres and you know I can't wear crap like that next to my skin.'

'Poor little diddums: you haven't got eczema, you've got delusions of grandeur,' Ed mocks.

'Will you both be quiet,' Dad says sternly. Dad never loses his rag but he's looking really fed up with them both. 'Here's a cup of tea, love,' he says to me. 'I'm sorry you got woken up. You worked so hard yesterday you deserve a bit of a lie in.'

I give him a grateful smile and then ask, 'What's going on?'

'Dad got us up early so we can go into town and find jobs,' Ed says. 'Spence says the supermarket where he works is desperate for staff. If we go and see the personnel officer this morning we'll probably be able to get started straight away.' He turns to Nell and adds crossly, 'You're not the only one whose plans are upset for today. I'd arranged to meet up with Ally.'

That wakes me up. I blink and swallow. *When did Ally and Ed get so friendly?*

'Ally? Why are you seeing her?' I ask in amazement. 'When did you arrange this? Don't you have any friends of your own?' I add accusingly. I don't mean to be horrid to him. I just don't want Ally worming her way into our lives.

Ed scowls at me and says, 'You don't have a monopoly on her. She doesn't have to ask your permission to talk to other people. As a matter of fact she sent me a text asking if I wanted to go to the coast. She's got a surfboard. It would have been so cool. I'd love to learn surfing. Sorry if she prefers my company to yours,' he adds sarcastically.

'I don't want to see her,' I mutter miserably. I can't believe he thinks I am jealous. 'I just don't know why you want to bother with her . . .' I add.

He ignores me and turns back to Dad. 'It's not fair. I don't want to work either. But at least I'm not like Nell—throwing her dummy out the pram at the thought of serving the *hoi polloi*.'

'I'm not throwing anything,' Nell says crossly. 'I just want a job I enjoy. Spence may like the supermarket but it doesn't mean I want to work there. He thinks it's great because he gets a discount and the chance to buy cheap food. But we're not reduced to that surely?' She looks towards Dad with a desperately plaintive expression.

'Is Spence really poor then?' I ask. I don't want to think about rich-bitch Ally luring Ed with her expensive toys like a spider with a fly—it's making me feel really stressed. So instead I concentrate on this bit of heart-rending information about Spence. 'I thought he said he had a dad in America who works for the Federal Government?'

'He has and his father does support them up to a point. But he sends only a certain amount of maintenance and, when it runs out, there's no more. His father has got a new wife and family to support—you have to see it from his point of view—he doesn't have endless income.'

'But that's so awful!' I say. There is a tightness in my throat at the thought of Spence not having enough money. I want to win the lottery and give half to him. I want him to be rich and happy and not have to work somewhere for a discount and the chance to buy dented tins. 'But I thought Spence said his mother works full time?' I add, managing to stop my voice from wobbling only with an effort.

'She works in a clothes shop,' Nell says flatly.

'So I suppose she doesn't earn very much . . .' I say.

'Most of what she earns goes on herself. She spends a fortune on glad rags and cosmetics,' Nell says.

'You're a fine one to talk,' Ed says nastily to her. Then he turns to me. 'Well, Alice, now you've got the low-down on Spence and his family's finances, perhaps we can get back to our own problems.' He gives me a withering look. He's full of hell this morning—raw with disappointment because of his cancelled date with Ally.

The whole idea of her getting his number and asking him out is weird. Why is she doing it? She's older than him and just not his type. But then Spence isn't Nell's type either. Maybe I have a lot to learn about how the world of grown-up attraction works. The thought of Ed and Ally getting friendly makes me feel sick. I don't want her hanging around my family. I want her to disappear.

'Are things very bad for us?' I ask Dad. Things seem very bad for me, but I want to know how things stand for the rest of them.

'Not tragic. Just a bit difficult,' Dad says calmly. 'It's bad timing Mum being made redundant with the twins going off to university. But we'll manage.' He turns to Nell and says gently: 'Don't work at the super-market if it will make you unhappy. All I will say is that you do need to get some kind of paid employment soon and save as much as you can.'

He then turns back to me and says, 'I'm sorry, Alice, but the twins working means you are stuck with helping Gary.' I can see that Dad is concerned, and I don't want to make it any harder for him, so I force a smile.

'I'll be fine. There aren't many customers at the moment so I can do my course-work at the same time. Don't worry about me,' I add cheerfully. It's all a front because I don't feel cheerful. I am deeply fed-up about not going to Italy and being stuck in the shop. Gary comes in only three days a week—for the rest of the time I will have to do all the work on my own. 'Mum will be at home. It'll be fun,' I add.

Dad meets my eyes and gives me a quick smile. I don't suppose I've deceived him for a moment. But I can see that he is grateful that I'm not having a tantrum like the twins. Thankfully they soon set off, the twins still bickering, and Dad looking tired. He can't stand arguments—he likes peace and quiet and there's a fat chance of that in this family at the moment.

I am left alone with Mabel and my breakfast. While I eat my cornflakes Mabel comes and rests her chin on my knee. It's as if she knows I am feeling low.

I take Mabel for a walk and, when I get back, Mum is up. She seems a bit dazed, as if she can't quite believe that she's at home on a working day.

'Gary phoned,' she says. 'He's ill and can't work.'

'Ill?' I echo. In all the years that Gary has worked for Gramps he's never been ill. 'That's a drag. Did he say what was wrong with him or how long he would be off?'

'No. He sounded most strange,' Mum says. 'I didn't like to question him.'

'I better go and water the greenhouses and open the shop,' I say. 'Although it's much too hot for gardening and we won't get any customers.'

'I'm going to tidy the house and do the washing,' Mum says decisively. 'I'll strip the beds,' she adds. She starts to pull out Gramps's ancient washing machine. 'Do you know how this works?' she asks me.

'Not really,' I say.

'You've got enough to do anyway,' Mum says. 'I'll bring you a coffee in a while.'

I water all the plants in the greenhouses. It takes me ages. Mabel sits in the shade and watches me. We don't have a single customer. At eleven o'clock— bored with my history book—I go back to the kitchen hoping for some freshly brewed coffee, hot toast, and company.

The kitchen table is still cluttered with the break-fast things. Mum has positioned the washing machine next to the sink and around it are piles of unwashed sheets, duvet covers, and towels. Mum's face is red and she's blinking back tears. I can tell she's really stressed because she talks to me in Italian and gestures with her hands.

84

'It's so, so crazy. Why does your gramps still have this dreadful old twin tub,' she raves. 'It should be in a museum—or taken to the tip. Surely, in the name of heaven, your father doesn't do all our washing in it? I can't get it to fill with water, let alone anything else. I shall have to drive into town and take everything to the launderette.'

'Oh dear, Dad always uses it,' I say glumly. 'There must be a special knack. He whizzes everything through, rinses them in the sink, and then spins them.'

'It must take hours,' Mum says with disbelief. 'Surely he changes the water?'

'No,' I say with surprise.

'How very unhygienic,' Mum says grimly. And I can see another family row brewing. Poor old Dad—why is everything so awful at the moment?

I clear the table and make us two mugs of instant coffee. I had hoped to sit in the kitchen with Mum and have a bit of a chat, but she says, 'Aren't you going back to the shop?'

'I can see if any customers arrive from here,' I say, positioning myself by the kitchen window.

'I think I'll have mine outside,' Mum says. And she disappears out of the door. I watch her cross the yard and walk to the end of the garden. I gulp my coffee. I've made it too strong and it leaves a bitter taste in my mouth.

I lock the shop door and follow Mum. She is standing in the shade of the jumping stones, leaning

85

on an old apple tree, smoking a long white cigarette. Her coffee mug is on the ground. She hates instant so I don't suppose she will drink it. Her movements are jerky as she smokes. She doesn't look as if she's enjoying it. Watching her smoke is like watching a hamster on a wheel. There is something futile and sad about it.

I walk up behind her and when I speak I make her jump. 'I thought you said you'd given up?' I say, trying to sound laid back and cool and not accusing. But it doesn't work.

'I had. I mean—I will.'

'Dad will be gutted if he finds out,' I say. 'You can't say you've given up and then still do it.'

'It soothes my nerves,' she says. And she takes one long drag on the cig and throws it on the ground. Then she grinds at it with her heel as if she hates it.

'Why don't you throw them all away? You wouldn't waste money by buying any more, would you?' I say.

She gives me a desperate kind of look.

'Mum, please.'

'Yes, yes, I will. But not today—not with everything that is going on . . .' She shrugs her shoulders and there is a world of meaning in that one gesture.

I go back to the shop and my history book. I can't shout at her today. She looks so defeated. And I can't tell Dad that she's smoking because he'll be upset; or Nell, because she'll fly into a fury because Mum is wasting money when she has to work in a shop; or Ed, because he'll say it's Mum's choice. I sit for ages trying to think of the best thing to do. I decide to get hold of some of the anti-smoking literature we were given at school and make Mum read it. If she looks at a couple of black lungs and harrowing descriptions of lung diseases, it might put her off. It certainly worked for me.

I shall have to wait until I get a day off and can go into town. Goodness knows when that will be. Thanks to Gary I am well and truly lumbered. I sit in the sweltering shop, listening to the buzz of insects and the lowing of the cows in the fields. I feel as if I am in prison. And ahead of me is a long, long sentence in solitary confinement.

Nell and Ed come home in the cool of the early evening. They have bundles of bright orange clothes with them and dinky white hats and name badges. They both have jobs at the supermarket.

I follow Nell upstairs. I've decided I will tell her about Mum smoking and ask her to help me. I would also like to talk to her about Ally. I want to ask her to warn Ed not to get friendly with Ally because she's bogus and creepy. But I don't know how to do it tactfully. Both she and Ed seem to think Ally is great. I don't understand it.

Nell is busy throwing the orange clothes onto hangers and shoving them into her wardrobe. There is such rage in her body language that I don't venture past the doorway just in case she chucks something at me. And I decide this is not the time to tell her about Mum. Instead I ask in a chatty, conversational voice, 'Which counter are you on?'

'Bread and cakes,' she snaps.

'That'll be nice. Croissants and bagels and lovely Danish pastries—you'll like that,' I say encouragingly.

'The smell makes me feel sick,' she says.

'Well, it won't be for ever, will it?' I say optimistically. Although in truth the rest of the holidays stretch before me like an endless desert.

'If I thought it was I'd shoot myself,' Nell announces, and when she turns to face me I see tears rolling down her face.

I move across and give her a hug. Nell manages to look beautiful even when crying. The curve of her cheek, heavy-lidded eyes, and sorrowful mouth remind me of a sculpted angel I once saw in Florence.

'Come on,' I cajole. 'It's crap for all of us, you know. I was stuck in the shop all day. And I had to water the greenhouses three times. I felt as if I was being deep fried in batter. Just think, in a few weeks you'll be off to London—it will be amazing.'

'Yes,' she says, but she isn't really listening to me.

'It must be nice for you to be working with Spence. Do you get to have lunch breaks together?' I ask, carefully, politely. It is quite an ordeal for me to say his name to Nell and keep my voice neutral.

'Don't be ridiculous,' she says. 'Have you any idea of the vastness of that great temple to shopping? And how many shifts it is possible to be on? Mealtimes and breaks bear no resemblance to the real world.

People are eating all day and having coffee breaks at noon. Spence is working overtime.' For some reason that makes her tears gush forth and she wipes her eyes with her palms.

'Nell, don't cry. Mum cried today about the washing machine.' My voice wavers. 'I hate it when everyone cries.'

Nell stares at me for a long moment. Her eyes seem very dark, shadowed and hurt.

'It's not just the job in the supermarket, is it?' I say.

She shakes her head.

'Is it Mum losing her job and us not going to Italy?'

She shakes her head again. And then she blurts out: 'It's Spence. I just don't understand him. Everything is so good between us and he's got the chance to go to university in London. We've got the chance be together for the next three years in the capital. But he's so vague and full of stupid dreams. I just wish he was older and more committed.'

'Maybe you wouldn't like him so much if he was older and more committed,' I say a bit desperately. 'Maybe he's special to you because of his songs and his clothes and the way he lives his life. Maybe you wouldn't like him so much if he changed. He'd be more like everyone else then, wouldn't he?'

Nell stares at me for what seems like ages—then she laughs; it's only a tiny laugh and it ends as a little sob, but I can see her mood changing like sunshine appearing after a storm.

'How perceptive you are, Alice. You're growing up, aren't you?' She says this wonderingly, as if she thought I'd be an annoying little sister all my life.

Then she hugs me. 'I think I can change him. And I think I'll like him more than ever when he's more like me. He needs someone to organize him. His mother just lives her own life. She doesn't bother much with either of the boys. Spence needs someone to look after him and give his life direction.'

She doesn't add, 'And I am just the right person to do it,' but it is as if I can see those words in her head.

'Nell, how can you change someone? I don't mean if they are doing something you don't like, I mean more than that. If they are doing something wrong, bad for them. What's the best way to get them to see the light?' At that moment I am thinking about Mum and Ed. I don't have a clue how to approach either of them. Maybe Nell can help.

'You change someone by being an example and a mentor to them—nagging won't do it,' Nell says. She hugs me again. 'If Spence loves me enough he'll do what I want, won't he?'

'Yes, I should think so,' I say uncertainly. I am sure in my own mind that Mum loves me. She tells me she does all the time. Every time she phones me or comes home she says the words. But does she love me enough to stop smoking if I ask her? I don't know. And if I'm not certain about Mum then I'm not confident about anyone. And I don't think I have any chance at all of changing Ed's mind about Ally. Life is difficult. One thing I do know is that I seem to have cheered Nell up. And that at least is something.

Chapter 9

The next week is an absolute nightmare. I should be packing my suitcase and getting on a plane to Italy where I would be fussed and hugged by my relations. Instead I am stuck in the shop.

Hannah and Chloe are busy getting ready to go away on holiday and haven't got time to come out to see me. I have blown any chance of friendship with Sam. And Mum is in the strangest mood and is no company at all. I am really fed up.

As if all that wasn't bad enough Mum starts blitzing Gramps's house. It is totally awful and embarrassing. We are meant to be looking after the house for him, not gutting it so he doesn't recognize it. Mum says the house is still in a mess from the party. But the party didn't go anywhere near the attic, the airing cupboard, or the pantry and she spends hours clearing them out. I suppose it's all the years she's had a high-powered stressful job. She can't switch off now.

Anyway, she goes on the rampage, and works from dawn till dusk at top speed. The house is horrible, full of bulging black bin-bags and the smell of bleach. It's actually quite a relief to hide in the shop and keep out of the way. I make loads of history notes because there's nothing else to do and no one to talk to but Mabel. I could quite easily die from loneliness if it wasn't for Gramps, who sends me lots of text messages and rings me on his mobile to tell me jokes.

When we get any customers I tell him exactly what they have bought and try to sound really positive. But customers are few and far between and the amounts of money I cash up in the evening are pathetically small.

I don't see Dad, Ed, or Nell. They are either working or sleeping. And consequently I never see Spence. I tell myself that this is good for me and I must forget all about him. And that each new day is the start of the rest of my life—a life in which he will play no part. But I find it impossible. My life is so boring . . . I don't have anything else to think about. Or at least nothing that's as fascinating as him.

By Monday morning of the second week I am so bored with sitting in the shop alone that I find myself wishing that someone, anyone, would come by to relieve the tedium. Gramps always says to be careful what you wish for and it proves to be true. A posh car pulls too fast into the yard on a cloud of acrid dust—like the baddie in a pantomime.

'Oh, flipping hell! What on earth does she want?' I mutter, as Ally gets out of her swanky Beetle and waves to me. She looks cool and comfortable in a white linen suit, and her hair has been cut close to her head so that it is as smooth and dark as sealskin.

She gets a briefcase out of the back of her car and walks over to the shop, waving to me with her free hand. 'Hi, Alice—how are you?' she asks, beaming at me.

'Hot,' I say unsmilingly.

'It is warm,' she says with a shrug. She looks happy, pleased with herself. 'I saw Ed earlier,' she adds. 'He said the air con is down in the store and it's terrible in there.'

'Oh dear,' I say. I am too overheated and cross to care much one way or the other. I have enough problems of my own without worrying about Ed. I just wish he wasn't talking to Ally at all.

Ally puts the briefcase down on the counter and begins to unzip it. 'Look, Alice, I know you're having trouble with your computer and you've got work to do, so I brought you this. It's my spare one. Daddy-o updates mine every year so I have a brand new model.'

She unfastens the case and lifts out a tiny laptop computer. 'It's got all the design programs I use on my course. You'll have a wild time playing around with it. Let me show you what you can do with Art Wizard. It's cool as ice.'

She lifts the lid, presses a switch and the screen lights up to a lurid green, like an evil genie. I back away from her. 'No,' I say loudly. 'I don't want it.'

My tone of voice makes her stop what she is doing. She glances up and gives me an understanding smile as she says, 'Hey, don't panic. You can do whatever you want with it. It's yours. It doesn't matter if you drop it or wipe everything off the hard drive. I'll be able to sort it out. I'll give you my mobile number and if you have a glitch you can ring me. It's a mean machine. I promise you, you'll love it. I checked with Ed about your printer and I've reprogrammed it so it's compatible. You'll zip through your work in no time at all—and you can do lots of graphics to make it look ni—'

I don't let her finish. She's going off like a salesman desperate for commission. I get the feeling she's really targeting me. 'I really don't want it,' I say. I feel absolutely desperate. I can't bear the thought of borrowing something from her and everyone assuming we are best buddies. I don't want to be friends with her. I don't know what stupid game she's playing but I'm not joining in.

I wish I had the courage to ask her why she was camping up on the crag and spying on us. And why she gatecrashed the party and is so keen to get in with everyone. It's just so creepy!

'Well, I'll leave it here and you can use it if you want to,' she says.

'NO!' I am nearly shouting now. 'Take it away.'

'OK, OK, keep your hair on.' She grins, as if I amuse her. 'I didn't realize you were such a technophobe. It's only a tiny computer—not a dirty bomb,' she adds with a snigger.

To my relief she shuts everything down and zips up the briefcase. 'I'll just go and say "Hi" to your mum,' she says airily.

'She's terribly busy. I don't think she'll want to see

you,' I say quickly. I know that I am being rude and part of me is ashamed that I feel such strong dislike for her and am acting so badly. Mum would be shocked and annoyed. 'She's cleaning and she hates to be interrupted,' I add lamely.

Ally laughs again. She's not taking me seriously at all. 'See you, Alice,' she says as she goes out of the door.

'Not if I see you first,' I say under my breath. She's so cocky, so sure of herself. Why does she think Mum would want to see her anyway?

I'm paid out for my rudeness and spiteful thoughts. Customers arrive: two ancient old ladies in an antique Morris Minor which I imagine they've had from new. They come into the shop and cluck around slowly like two gentle brown hens, poring over the gifts, cards, and plants as if it's Santa's Grotto.

And while I am imprisoned in the shop with them I see Mum and Ally come out of the back door together. They are carrying mugs of coffee and talking and laughing like a pair of schoolfriends. They disappear down to the apple trees at the end of the garden, well out of my sight. They've gone for a fag—even a half-wit could work that out. Mum will come back smelling of peppermints and perfume and think I am too slow to realize that she's been smoking. My jaw is clenched with anger. The fact that Mum is smoking is bad enough but doing it with Ally seems to make it a thousand times worse. I imagine them joking about how I mustn't find out because I am such an immature spoilsport. I could cry with rage. Everyone in my family seems to prefer Ally to me.

When Ally finally leaves I refuse to wave to her and even though she toots her horn I just look away. I know I am being a baby but I hate her more every time I see her.

The two old ladies buy lots of plants and some flower pots but I am too miserable to care. I stay in the shop sulking until Mum calls me in for lunch. Even then there is no comfort. All the time we are having our sandwiches Mum goes on and on about how she has found a jar of jam in the pantry that is dated Aug '84. I get the feeling she is never going to shut up about it.

'I don't suppose Gramps was going to eat it,' I say miserably. 'I expect he was saving it for sentimental reasons. Gran must have made it.' I am quite tearful at the thought. And I sniff so loudly that Mum looks up. She leans over the table and touches my cheek with her hand.

'*Poverina!* You poor darling,' she says. 'You have been stuck in that shop for days on end in this terrible heat. You must have a couple of days off. Dad and I will look after everything. Why don't you go out with your friends tomorrow, and the next day I'll take you over to see Gramps. You'd like that, wouldn't you?'

I nod, unable to speak I am so happy. Two days away from the shop sounds like absolute bliss.

'I'll ring Hannah and Chloe and arrange to go shopping,' I say. I have littered the house with anti-smoking leaflets which I found in my PSE folder. Even though they have all ended up neatly stacked and returned to my room I am not going to give up my fight to stop Mum smoking. Especially now she is sneaking off for a fag with Ally, of all people. That is an extra added incentive to get Mum to kick the habit. 'While I'm in town would you like me to get you some nicotine patches? They are very good to help you stop smoking,' I say, trying to sound casual and not desperate.

'No thank you, Alice,' she says sternly. 'I need nothing like that.'

I feel as if she has slapped me and any pleasure at my shopping trip dies instantly. I feel as if Ally manages to cast a poisonous net over my life even when she's not around.

I have to get the bus into town to meet Hannah and Chloe because no one is around to give me a lift. By the time I get there I am really hot. I would rather have gone swimming but Han and Chloe have last minute shopping to do for their hols.

Before we begin our tour of the make-up counters we go to The Continental to treat ourselves to a coffee and a scone. Hannah and Chloe are full of endless stories about Alfie and Greg. In contrast I have nothing exciting to tell them: a hopeless crush on my sister's boyfriend, a nearly romance with Sam—over before it began—and a really nasty gate-crasher at Nell and Ed's party are hardly good gossiping material.

All I can think of to report to them is: 'Mabel fell in love with a collie dog and he sat outside the house all night and howled for her. I wish someone loved me enough to do that.' For some reason this sends them off into hysterics and I find I am giggling too.

'I wish you were coming with us to Tenerife,' Hannah says.

'It's just not the same without you,' Chloe adds. 'We don't have half as many laughs when it's just the two of us. Next year we'll all try to go away together, shall we?'

We are busy having a fantasy holiday discussion—planning exotic destinations that we would like to visit without the restriction of parents—when I get this nasty prickle down my spine. I am being watched. Someone is staring at me.

I shift in my seat. Then slowly I turn. Sitting at a table on the other side of the café is Ally. She must have been watching me because as soon as I turn she raises her hand in a salute. Then, to my horror, she gets to her feet, picks up her handbag and comes over to our table.

'Hi, Alice,' she says. 'Your mum told me you were in town and I'd probably find you here. Do you mind if I join you?'

Chapter 10

There is a beat of silence. 'This is Ally,' I mutter. 'A friend of Ed's,' I add. It pains me to call her that. But she's certainly no friend of mine. And I can't very well introduce her as a weirdo stalker who is following me around and really getting on my nerves. She appears to have Ed well and truly in her fan club. Why can't she leave me alone?

'This is Hannah and Chloe,' I mumble. No one seems to have noticed that my mood has changed. Hannah and Chloe are smiling and saying 'Hi'.

'Have you girls finished lunch?' Ally asks, settling herself down at our table and looking at our empty plates. We haven't had lunch. The Continental is too expensive for us to have more than a small coffee and a scone. 'Let me treat you to a coffee and a cake,' Ally adds. 'My allowance from my father has just arrived and I'm flush. The chocolate banana cake in here is the best I've ever had outside of the States.'

'Oh no, really, we're fine. Thank you,' I try to say. But Ally takes no notice.

She orders large American coffees and chocolate cake for us all. It will cost a bomb. And when the great fat gooey slices arrive at the table no one but me can resist them. Anyway it would be so rude to refuse . . . But I can't eat my cake; I just stare down at it. The rich sickly smell makes me feel quite ill. I can't sit here with Ally and eat cake that she has bought. Knowing that she found out where I was and followed me is making me feel queasy.

'Oh, I shouldn't do this just before I have to get into my bikini,' Hannah says delightedly, licking her cake fork. Chloe is busy telling Ally all about their holiday. Ally's splashed out some money and bought herself some friends. But she hasn't bought me.

'You can have my cake,' I say to Han, pushing the plate across the table towards her. 'I'm off to the loo.'

I don't go to the Ladies, there's no network in there. Instead I run out into the street and dodge into the doorway of M&S.

Once again I ring Sam without thinking about it beforehand. 'Sam—this is Alice. I've met that girl who came to the party—Ally—the other Alice. She's following me. It's stressing me out! I need help!' I tell him breathlessly.

'What! She's followed you to Italy?' he asks, bemused.

'I'm not in Italy. I'm in town—outside M&S.'

'What happened to Italy?'

'It got cancelled.'

'I'll be down in five. Don't go away. I'll be right there,' he says. It's great that he understands straight away and I don't have to go into long explanations.

When I first see him, weaving through the shoppers on his bike, I suddenly recall in graphic detail how it felt when he kissed me. And despite the sweltering heat a shiver runs across my neck and turns my arms all goose bumpy. I am pleased to see him and dismayed by this reaction in equal measure. The way he makes me feel is really, really confusing.

'Hi, is she still here?' he asks eagerly.

'Yes, she's sitting in The Continental with Hannah and Chloe telling them tall stories about her wonderful life and her rich father. They're at a corner table scoffing cake. Have a look through the window. You can't miss her. She's the one dressed all in red with very short dyed black hair and lots of earrings and jewellery.'

He moves his bike so that it is leaning against the wall, walks past the café and then doubles back to me. 'Got her! What a freak. I'll wait here, shall I? Then I can follow her and see where she goes. I might get a glimpse of the sick granny, you never know.'

'She's been out to the garden centre hanging around me and Mum. And she's getting really pally with Ed. I don't know what she's up to. She found out from my mum that I was in town. I don't know what she's after and why she's so interested in us. But I wish she'd go away . . .'

'I'll see what I can find out for you,' he says kindly. 'I'll suss where she's staying and do a bit of snooping.'

We both try really hard not to look at each other but it doesn't work. In the end we just stare—our eyes unable to look away. It seems like only seconds ago that we were together at the crag kissing, when in reality it has been days. Yet I know we are both thinking about it again. Eventually he stops staring at my mouth and says, 'So what happened to Italy?'

'My mother has been made redundant. She's fallen out with her family in Italy so we're not going there ever again. It's shit. We've got no money so Nell and Ed have had to get proper jobs and I'm lumbered with watering the greenhouses and serving in the shop.'

'It beats course-work and revision,' he says.

'I have to do that at the same time. And Gary, who's meant to work at the garden centre, has a mystery illness and hasn't shown his face for days. So I don't have anyone to help me.'

'I could come out and give you a hand, if you like,' he says casually, as if he is offering me a coffee or a bag of chips instead of a lifeline.

'OK,' I say, trying to be just as casual. 'I've got a day off tomorrow—Dad is looking after the shop so I can go to see my gramps—but the day after would be great.'

'I'll come over early,' he says. And then he suddenly snakes his arm around my waist and pulls me against him—wrapping himself all around me—just as if we are lovers. 'Don't turn round, stay still, she's just coming out of The Continental now,' he murmurs into my ear. 'She's walking down the street very slowly. And she's staring around at everyone as if she's looking for someone. I bet she's looking for you!'

A shiver runs right down my back when he says that!

'I'll stay here for a couple of minutes and then I'll go after her,' he whispers.

It's not at all unpleasant being crushed against him. He smells nice and his breath against my ear tickles delightfully. But my nanosecond of enjoyment is cut brutally short.

'Alice!' says a surprised, shocked voice, and I freeze. Sam releases me quickly and we both turn guiltily, like naughty children caught pinching sweets.

Hannah and Chloe are standing and staring at us. 'We've been looking everywhere for you,' Hannah says pointedly to me.

'We thought you'd been abducted, or got lost; we were worried,' Chloe says, staring at Sam as if he's an alien.

'This is Sam,' I mumble.

'We were having a coffee before she saw you and got carried away,' Chloe says to Sam, as if it's his fault I ran out on them. Then they glance at each other and start to smirk. I can see what they are thinking: What a joke, sleepy old Alice sneaking off to snog a boy—and in the centre of town where everyone can see!

I give Sam an agonized look. He grins at me sympathetically and says, 'I'll let you get on with your shopping. Speak to you later.'

Hannah and Chloe quiz me like mad about him. Is he my boyfriend? Where did I meet him? How long have I been going out with him? How many dates? Where and when?

I know they are disappointed by my replies. I can't tell them that he kissed me once and it was mind-blowingly wonderful—but that I turned him down. It sounds crazy. I wish I could talk to them about Spence and Sam and my innermost feelings. But I feel too confused to put any of it into words. My thoughts are in too much of a muddle.

Sam phones me as soon as I get through the door at home. 'I followed that weird girl to a hotel—a rather posh one behind the conference centre. Her pink Beetle with the personalized number plate was parked there.'

'That's crazy. Why is she staying in a hotel? She's meant to be staying with her gran.'

'Nothing adds up, does it?' he says.

'No . . . And I suppose it's too much to hope we've seen the last of her. She's bound to turn up here again.'

'Ring me when she does,' he says. 'And I'll see you the day after tomorrow.'

My brain is buzzing with unanswered questions about Ally. It's a relief to help Mum get supper ready and have something else to think about. 'Two extra,' Mum says to me as I am getting the cutlery out.

'Two?' I say with surprise.

'Yes, Ed phoned. Ally is meeting him from work and giving him a lift home and Nell is bringing Spence. I invited them to eat with us.'

105

Ally's everywhere today. Stalking me—meeting Ed. Her coming here again is bad news. I really am sick of her, with her sly smile and ingratiating manner. My heart sinks at the thought of having to sit through a meal with her. I tell myself that I must try to find out about her background and why everything about her is such a mystery. I wish Sam was here. He's much more on the ball than me. It makes me feel dizzy thinking about it. I'm not detective material.

To make it worse the very thought of Spence coming for supper, and being in his company for any length of time, eclipses every sensible thought in my head and sends me into emotional free-fall. My hands start to shake so much that the spoons and forks jiggle about. I finish setting the table and then dash up to my room.

My mind is racing. Top priority—I mustn't be too obvious. Getting changed, putting on more make-up, and redoing my hair would look suspicious. I gaze at my reflection in the mirror. I look all right. I washed my hair and curled it before I went shopping. I am wearing my best clothes. This is just about as good as it gets for me.

Then reality hits me. It doesn't matter what I look like—Spence won't ever feel anything for me. He's in love with Nell. He loves her for her personality and her intellect, because she's fun to be with and sharp witted. I'll never be like that . . .

I plait my hair and take off my best clothes. I put on my oldest T-shirt and a pair of shorts. I could pass for a ten year old. I use a face wipe and take off my mascara. I want this to really hurt. Maybe when I'm hurting I won't love him any more.

The two cars arrive and they get out and stand around in the yard talking. Even though there are only four of them they sound like a big laughing crowd, a gathering or a party. Dad always says that if Nell was ever stranded in a desert, within twenty-four hours she would have a group of friends and a party going.

I take Mabel for a walk. I sneak out through the front door so I don't have to see anyone. Ally is here, so later I will ring Sam. But I will wait until I have something to report. The thought of speaking to him, and the prospect of him coming over to help me in the shop, is like a light at the end of a dark tunnel. It cheers me up.

The evening is so hot that I take Mabel down to the river so I can go paddling. The water is wonderfully cold and clear. I poke around in the green weeds, which flow like mermaid hair over the stones, and disturb a brown trout in a deep pool.

When I get back to the house everyone is sitting out in the garden. They are talking and laughing about Mum's spring-cleaning, and how many bin-bags of rubbish she has removed from the attic. I don't think it's funny. There might have been stuff up there that Gramps wanted to keep. I haven't dared tell Gramps what she has been up to. I think he might be really upset.

'Now you're back, Alice, we'll eat, shall we? We've been waiting for you,' Mum says.

'What have you been up to, little sis?' Spence asks me.

'Playing with mud pies by the look of her,' Nell says.

'I took Mabel to the river. It was lovely and cool and shady down there.'

Spence smiles at me but I look away quickly. I can see that he thinks I am funny. And that's not what I want.

'It's been like an oven in the store today. It was great to come home in Ally's car,' Ed says. 'She let me drive,' he adds, smiling across at her.

'I wish I could employ you as a chauffeur,' she replies with a grin. 'I am really fed up with not being able to have a glass of wine with meals. I don't drink at all when I'm driving, you see,' she adds primly.

'Well done, that's the only way to do it,' Dad says approvingly.

'And are you insured for any driver? That's amazing,' Nell says. 'It must cost a fortune.'

As we troop into the kitchen I hear Ed say to Mum, 'Would it be all right for Ally to stay the night? We thought we'd go to the pub and it means she can have more than lemonade to drink.'

'Of course it's all right,' Mum says. 'It's very sensible of her not to take risks when she's driving. I'll make up a bed in the spare room.'

'Thanks,' Ed says gratefully.

I sit opposite Ed and Ally. I have decided to make myself watch her and force myself to ask her questions. 'How's your gran?' I ask. I am trying to think of a way to talk about the hotel behind the conference centre. Because she can't be staying there and with her gran, can she?

'She's over in Scarborough, convalescing. It gives me a bit of a break from looking after her, so it's worked out really well,' Ally says smugly.

'So you're not staying with her at the moment?' I ask, but Ally doesn't reply.

Annoyingly Nell butts in and I don't have a chance to ask anything else. Nell pours us all some of her homemade lemonade. She concocted it from a recipe she found in a magazine. I think it's rather too sharp (a bit like Nell herself) but I don't like to ask for a spoonful of sugar. Nell proceeds to tell us in exact detail how she made the lemonade. Just in case, some time in the future, we might want to poison our friends and family with a taste that could disguise arsenic.

Ally goes on for ages about how wonderful it is and asks Nell to write down the recipe for her. Nell is so pleased about this it's pathetic. Can't she see that Ally is greasing up to her? I wonder why Ally wants everyone to like her so much? She's making such a fuss of Ed it's embarrassing. You'd think he was the best friend she'd ever had.

I stare at Ed for a while, because it stops me looking at Spence. I've never really thought about it before, but it must be hard being Nell's twin. He's always in the shadow of her personality and intelligence. Even in looks he isn't in her league. Her hair is naturally blonde, his just light brown. He does have nice dark eyes—we get those from Mum. And all the bits of his face are in the right place. But he's not drop-dead-gorgeous or anything. And he's not used to girls who are older than him making up to him as if he's Superman and letting him drive their fancy cars. He's kind of lit up about it. It's sickening to see it.

As soon as we've finished supper Ed and Nell rush off to get ready to go out. I hear them at the top of the stairs quarrelling about who can have the bath-room first.

'You and me will do the washing-up, shall we, little sis?' Spence says to me, giving me one of his lovely smiles.

If I was sensible I would say 'No'. I could make the excuse that the greenhouses need another watering. I could say I've got a toothache, a headache, a backache, but of course I don't do the sensible thing. I pout at him, like a ghastly cute kid in an American sit-com, and say, 'Let me wash the dishes, please? I hate drying.'

And so we are left alone in the kitchen together. He teases me about making too many bubbles with the washing-up liquid, and then he talks to me about his band and the songs he's writing. And it all makes my heartache much, much worse: because he's being sweet to me and I love him very much.

110

He makes coffee. He really concentrates while he measures out the beans. It's heaven watching him. The result is beautiful: dark brown, thick and rich. I pour it carefully into the best cups, put them on a tray with a jug of milk and a bowl of sugar, and carry it out to Mum and Dad and Ally.

Mum smiles at me. 'I was telling Ally that we are visiting Gramps tomorrow and she says she'd love to come along and meet him. Won't that be lovely?' Mum says.

The tray falls from my hands; the cups (thankfully) bounce on the lawn, but I watch Spence's lovely coffee stain the sun-dried grass and then quickly disappear into the baked ground. Mabel tries to help by licking up the sugar and wagging her tail.

Behind me I can hear Nell saying to Spence in a cross voice, 'Why on earth did you let her carry the tray? She's so clueless—she'd trip over a pin.'

And I just stand like an idiot and stare at Mum.

Chapter 11

I say a wasp stung me. Everyone assumes I
dropped the tray because of that. Mum tells
Nell off for being unkind and finds some sting
relief that I smear on my arm, although there is
nothing to see.

Spence pats my shoulder and tells me not to worry.
Then he makes more coffee. This time Dad carries it
out. I sit like a zombie, unable to speak. I wish I
could tell them the truth about why I dropped the
tray. It was all because of Ally. She was sitting there
with such a smug look on her face . . . so darned
pleased with herself. And I thought: She is staying
in my house, coming to meet my gramps, and all
because of a stupid lie that I told.

I've tried to untell it—but it hasn't worked. I want
to stand up now and denounce her as a liar and a
fraud. But it seems impossible. Now she is Ed's newest,
bestest friend, liked by everyone—except me.

Even while I am thinking these thoughts she is on
a charm offensive with Mum and Dad. She gets these
bottles of liqueur from her car that she's brought for
them. It's Calvados, or something fancy. Nell is
impressed.

'Just a little present—to thank you for your hospi-

112

tality,' Ally says. And Dad gets the best glasses from the dresser and Ally slops out great helpings of the stuff. Every time anyone takes a sip she tops their glass up. Spence won't have any because he is driving and I only stare at mine and refuse to touch it. Eventually he and I are the only ones who aren't giggling. The Calvados must be as strong as rocket fuel and Ally is making sure that everyone has plenty of it. I think it looks and smells vile. Anyway, I don't want anything of Ally's. Eventually I take my glass of Calvados into the kitchen and pour it down the sink. Then I exchange it for some apple juice so Ally won't have the chance to refill my glass. And when I have finished drinking the juice I make an excuse and go up to bed. I am sick of listening to everyone getting sloshed and laughing, and having fun with Ally.

I desperately try to ring Sam but I have no network. Then, in a futile attempt to calm myself down, I try to read my history book—but the words disappear into a river of print.

It's hours earlier than I normally go to bed, but as soon as I curl up under my sheet I fall asleep. My body clock must be in turmoil because at three o'clock I come to—fresh as a daisy and not sleepy at all.

The countryside is never silent and even at that time of the night there's plenty of noise coming in through my window. Sounds carry in darkness. If I listen hard I can hear the plop of frogs in the pond at the end of the garden. And down at the farm a cow is mooing a low mournful note. From the bushes under my window comes the insistent click of insects—crickets or grasshoppers. High up on the crag one owl hoots and another returns its call. And then I hear Mabel growl—a low-pitched rumbling in the back of her throat. It's the noise she makes before she starts barking. I sit up in bed and listen hard. Lambs from the river meadows are crying now in descant to the cow—but Mabel is silent.

My eyes are wide open and I am really awake. I realize that I am thirsty but apart from that I feel great. Bounding with energy in the middle of the night is a real waste. Maybe I should write up my history notes now, instead of waiting until the sweltering daytime when my eyelids close with weariness.

I slide out of bed and feel the cool floor under my feet. I don't think I can go back to sleep, but I can get my history work from the dining room and a drink from the kitchen and spend a useful hour making notes. If anything is likely to send me back to dreamland it's reading about the employment patterns of women during the First World War.

I tiptoe out onto the landing and down the stairs. The house is very dark. I manage the stairs using touch not sight. I can see more in the kitchen because moonlight is streaming in through the window. Mabel is lying in the middle of the floor busily eating something. She thumps her tail in welcome but doesn't move away from her trophy.

'What have you got?' I whisper to her. When I

bend over her she gives a little warning growl. 'Where did you get that from?' I say to her, because she is eating the remains of an enormous beefsteak. It's the kind of meat we rarely have and Mabel is fighting her way through it. She definitely doesn't want to share with me. I move back from her, my brain racing. *Someone is in the house. Someone has given Mabel the meat to keep her quiet . . .*

I open my mouth to scream. I want Dad and Ed to come running. I want Mum to phone the police. I want to wake up and find this is all part of a terrible nightmare. But some sixth sense warns me off making any noise at all. If I scream, whoever is in the house will know where I am. They will get to me before any of my family. They might have guns or knives. It would be safer to go back upstairs, wake Dad, and phone the police from there.

I leave Mabel to her steak and glide out into the hallway like a ghost. Now that I look closely I can see a thin line of light coming from underneath the dining room door. I move with agonizing slowness. I am afraid of making a noise. I am almost paralysed with fear.

It takes me ages to get across the hall. Every footstep is like walking on hot coals. I nearly make it to the bottom of the stairs but then Mabel lumbers out of the kitchen like a grizzly bear out hunting. She makes straight for the dining room door. She barges it open and walks in. I hear a horribly familiar cockney voice whisper, 'Have you finished that steak already, you greedy gal? You can have some more in just a tick. But shove off now.'

I am so shocked I stand stock-still, as if turned to stone, my mouth gaping open. There are so many emotions bombarding my head that I feel dizzy. All the unsettling feelings I have had about Ally since she first arrived at the party turn into one enormous whirlpool of fear. *Why is she down here? And what is she doing?*

For a moment I wish I had the courage to rush into the dining room and scream at her and ask her what the hell she is up to. But I can't do that. Instead I force myself to cross the hallway and peer into the room. Ally is sitting in front of the sideboard, and around her in tidy piles is the junk that is kept in there.

For an idiotic moment I wonder if she is trying to help Mum clean. There seems to be no other explanation why she should be turning out the contents of Gramps's sideboard. It's such a bizarre thing to do— especially in the middle of the night. Then I realize that she must be looking for something. Something of value? In Gramps's sideboard? What a hope! It is full of stuff that is too important to throw away but is worth nothing: stationery for the shop, Dad's invoice pad for his bills, bills that have been paid, receipts for equipment, guarantees, Mabel's pedigree papers, photographs, old library cards, school photographs, and paintings that date back to when Dad and Auntie Jess were at school. There are quite a few photo albums, with lots of loose photos fastened into the back with elastic bands. There's an old cream-cracker tin where important certificates are stored. And wrapped in a black silk cloth is the family Bible.

Mum has had her eye on the sideboard for the last couple of weeks. It's next on the list for the big clean up. *But why on earth is Ally going through all this stuff? Does she think we keep money in there?*

I watch her for a moment. She doesn't appear to be looking for money. She painstakingly opens and closes each page of the photo albums. Some dried flowers fall out and she very carefully picks them up and replaces them in the same page. I realize that she doesn't want anyone to ever know what she is doing—that is why she is being so particular.

Ally starts to put everything back. Mabel waits patiently, tail wagging. I hide myself behind the kitchen door. Money from the shop, such as it is, is kept in a cash box in the pantry. But the amounts we are making at the moment are pitiful and Ally doesn't appear to be short on cash. If half the stories about her rich father are true I would say she's rolling in it.

So what is she looking for? It's worse than just being nosy and having a snoop around. She's given everyone huge glasses of alcohol and kept Mabel quiet so she can have free run of the house. I feel as if we are under siege. And now she's got what she wants. She's right inside the house, on the prowl, while everyone but me is asleep. I am so scared now I am shaking like a leaf.

Ally comes into the kitchen—she is so close to me I could put out my hand and touch her. But I cringe back from her as if she is a viper. I close my eyes and try not to breathe.

I hear the sound of rustling plastic. 'There you are, good gal,' she says, and I know she is giving Mabel another slice of meat. I hear her unlocking the back door and the clink of keys. Then there is the unmistakable sound of the back door closing.

I count up to ten and then risk creeping out from my hiding place. I stand by the side of the kitchen window and watch her. She is unlocking the workshop. If she's looking for junk she's gone to the right place. Mum has stored all the bin-bags of rubbish from the loft in there.

I wipe my sweating face and hands on the kitchen towel and try to calm myself down. I must find out what Ally is up to. Mabel, the traitor, has retired to her bed. She obviously thinks that anyone who gives out steak must be her best friend.

I cross the yard in my bare feet and slide up to the workshop window. Ally is on her hands and knees. She is painstakingly going through the bags of rubbish: old clothes and books, some of Dad's toys from when he was a kid, an old sewing machine that belonged to Gran, bits of broken furniture. Ally is again piling it neatly, sorting methodically. She works fast, but not furiously. I am totally perplexed. More than anything I wish I had Sam here with me to see it. Not just because I'm terrified and could do with a hug. But because in the morning I might think I've dreamt it all.

I creep back to the house and go upstairs to bed. I am shivering from head to foot with nerves and determined not to go back to sleep. I am scared—but I am not sure what of. It is an unknown terror—not knowing who Ally is or why she is behaving like this. Whatever happens I am going to stay awake and guard my family. I hear Ally coming stealthily back up the stairs and the click of the spare room door as it closes.

Then the birds begin their dawn chorus. The night is nearly over—what a relief! I look at my clock. Dad will be up in half an hour. That is such a reassuring thought that, despite my best efforts to keep my eyes open, I start to doze off.

Chapter 12

I jolt into consciousness when Mum comes into my room carrying a mug of tea.

'We've all overslept. It's nearly eight o'clock. Dad's in a rush—he's got a job he wanted to start early,' Mum says. 'Are you all right, darling,' she asks, looking concerned. 'You look terrible. I wouldn't have let you have the Calvados if I'd known how strong it was. Have you got a hangover?'

'No, have you?'

'Just a bit of a headache,' she admits. 'Nell had four glasses and she's still asleep.'

I drink the tea and try to ring Sam. I want to speak to him so much I feel weak with longing. He doesn't answer his phone. I daren't leave anything on his voice-mail in case I start crying—or leave him an over-emotional message saying I need to speak to him NOW, and no one else in the world will do. I can't unscramble my feelings about Ally on my own. I need him to help me.

I go downstairs and try to eat some breakfast. Mum is making a picnic for us to take to Gramps. I keep thinking how awful it is that we are stuck with Ally for another day. I had been really looking forward to seeing Gramps but now it is all spoilt. I keep half

120

starting sentences. I want to tell Mum about what I saw last night. But now in the clear light of morning it seems crazier than ever. Mum might tell me I dreamt it all and am being silly—and if she does that I shall start to cry because my emotions feel red raw.

I keep ringing Sam but even his voice-mail is down. In desperation I sneak off into the sitting room and look his family up in the phone book so I can call him on his land line. They're not listed anywhere—they must be ex-directory. My eyes do fill up then and I sit for a moment and snivel. Why is Sam out of contact when I need him so much?

Ally doesn't come downstairs until we are due to leave. She looks like a ghoul with dark rings under her eyes. And she drinks three cups of black coffee and takes two Panadol while Mum is packing up the sandwiches.

'We can take Mabel with us, can't we? Gramps would love to see her. He always asks about her when he phones and tells me how much he is missing her,' I say. 'Although she's got awful wind this morning so she's not going to be the nicest travelling companion. I don't know what's wrong with her. She must have eaten something that has really disagreed with her. I do hope she hasn't been poisoned . . .' My words hang in the air for a moment like an unanswered question. 'If she was a human she'd probably have to go to hospital to have her stomach pumped out,' I add dramatically. And I give Ally a sharp stare as I say that—hoping for some response, some flash of guilt, but she just looks back at me blankly.

'Oh dear, poor Mabel, I wonder what she's eaten,' Mum says in alarm. 'Maybe we should give her a dose of Milk of Magnesia. She does look very blown up, doesn't she? And of course you can take her to see Gramps,' Mum adds kindly. 'Although she'll have to stay in the garden, especially as she's got a poorly tummy. You know how house-proud Auntie Jess is.'

I nod. Auntie Jess is lovely but her house gives me the creeps. It is unnaturally clean and tidy. No clutter, no books, no sign of human habitation: just cream carpets, white leather furniture, glass-topped, smear-free tables adorned with artificial flowers in hideous modern vases. Ally wouldn't find any sideboards full of family history or junk to go through in that house.

Even the plants in Auntie Jess's garden look as if they have been spaced out with a ruler and carefully colour coded so that everything matches. It's hard to believe that Gramps and Granny had two such totally different offspring as Dad and Auntie Jess. Dad hates gardens that are too regimented. He likes nothing better than a riot of colour and creepers. And he always says that a good garden should have a little bit of wilderness in a corner for the butterflies. The very mention of wilderness has Auntie Jess reaching for the weedkiller.

When we get to Auntie Jess's house Gramps is waiting for us in the garden. He's sitting under a shady tree with his walking sticks propped up against a small table. Mum introduces Ally as my friend. I can't speak for a few minutes because I am so upset and cross about this. I want to shout out that she's not my friend; she was up all night snooping around Gramps's house and she is weird and horrible. But my mouth feels as if it has been glued up. I can't make a sound. I just sit in icy silence, fuming.

Fortunately no one notices me because Mabel is making such a fuss. She is overjoyed to see Gramps and she dances around him barking and wagging her tail. And after Gramps has said 'hello' to her, she lies under his chair and looks up at him with adoring eyes.

Gramps's white hair has been cut very short and he looks smaller to me, as if not being able to work or walk has shrunk his whole skeleton. His eyes seem sad as he asks me how things are going at the garden centre.

'Alice has been such a help,' Mum says. 'Nell and Ed are working every hour they can, getting some savings for university. Alice has been in sole charge of the shop and made such a good job of it.'

Gramps nods his head and says, 'I know how hard you've been working. You are a good girl. How would I have managed without you? I'm afraid I've had bad news from Gary. He's given in his notice. Evidently he's got himself a job at Garden Heaven, the big new superstore on the main road. They've creamed off all my trade and now they've got Gary.'

'That's terrible!' Ally says heatedly. 'How can they take all your trade?'

'Quite easily, I'm afraid,' Gramps says sadly. 'It's a ruthless old world. Garden Heaven undercuts me on price every time and folk don't seem so interested in quality these days. It's all instant colour and decking in gardens, isn't it?'

'It stinks that they have been allowed to open a big mega-store so close to you. It's wrong—totally wrong. It's like thieving to put you out of business,' Ally says forcefully. 'They should be made to pay compensation or something for stealing your livelihood. And they shouldn't be allowed to pinch your staff. That's out of order. And that Gary must be a right scum-bag for going along with it. He wants his arse kicking. They all want their arses kicking,' she adds.

Gary doesn't seem much of a loss to me, but I suppose Gramps needs him for the heavy work. And I don't know why Ally is getting in such a stress about it all. She's looking really belligerent—as if she'd like to give Gary a bloody nose for running out on Gramps. I suppose she's the type of toughie who'd scrap with anyone over anything.

'When I'm back on my feet I shall have to think about what to do . . .' Gramps says with a small smile. 'I'm not ready for the scrap heap yet, not by a long way.'

'I should think not,' I say.

'You can't let Garden Heaven get away with it, not without a fight,' Ally says.

We all sit and stare around at the garden for a

while. I suppose we are thinking about our own problems. Ally is frowning. Her face is intense, as if she is planning to kidnap Gary and make him return to work for Gramps. I don't know why she's so het up about it all. It's nothing to do with her. It's not as if it is her Gramps who is in trouble. I wish she'd keep her nose out of our business. I wish we'd never talked about Garden Heaven and Gary.

No one speaks—I suppose we are all busy worrying. There's Gramps with his failing business and Mum with her lack of a job. And as for me! My problems run into a list: Spence has broken my heart, Sam is out of contact just when I really need him, and I am stuck with a stalker who seems to have an unnatural interest in anything to do with my family. It seems that Mabel is the only one who is trouble free and she is looking very pleased with herself.

Gramps pats my hand. 'I can see that you've taken great care of my Mabs.' He smiles as he adds, 'She's looking in the pink.'

'Yes, she's looking well, isn't she?' Mum says. 'Alice takes her for lots of walks and brushes her. And she was very careful with Mabel when she was in season.'

'Ah, we'll have our pedigree pups one day, won't we?' Gramps says smiling. 'You are a good lass, Alice, to look after Mabel as well as the shop. It's a lot of work for you.'

Ally turns to me and says, 'I'm off to the States for a couple of weeks. But when I get back I could give you a hand in the shop, you know. I'd love to do that.' She looks across at Gramps and says urgently, 'I really want to do something to help. I think it's so crap what's happened to you.'

I stare at her—confused—trying to collect my thoughts. I want to leap into the air and scream 'Yes!' because she is going away for two whole weeks. Two weeks when I don't have to think about her being up on the crag or sliming around Ed or turning up at the house. But I must be careful. I would rather share the shop with a venomous spider than with her. I must find a cast-iron reason why she can't help me or I am never going to be rid of her.

'My friend Sam is coming over tomorrow,' I say quickly. 'And he's going to help me for the rest of the holidays,' I add rashly. 'So I don't need anyone else. There really isn't work for three people. It would be a waste of time you coming over, honestly.'

'There must be something I could do?' Ally says, giving me a long dark-eyed stare.

'I don't need any help but Sam,' I say firmly. 'We've got school work to do as well. So having someone else around would be a distraction,' I add.

'Are you sure that Sam is going to be able to come over every day to help?' Mum asks giving me a warning glance. 'It's a huge commitment.' She obviously feels that I've snubbed Ally.

'Yes, he's coming over every single day. It's all planned. We've got a work rota organized,' I lie swiftly, spurred on by desperation. Even if Sam doesn't come near me after tomorrow I'm not having Ally helping me. No fear!

'That's very good of your friend Sam. I shall pay you both, of course,' Gramps says.

'No, no!' I am nearly shouting. This is getting worse and worse. Why is everything so complicated? It's all bloody Ally's fault. 'Honestly, Gramps, we don't need to be paid. The arrangement suits us. You see, we need some peace and quiet to do our revision and course-work. It's no trouble at all to keep an eye on the shop at the same time,' I say quickly.

'Well, it will be nice for you to have some company. I've been so busy,' Mum says, and she glances at Gramps as she says this. And I hope she is feeling guilty for turning out his attic and pantry.

Ally butts in and starts talking and I don't want to listen. So I get up and begin to mooch around the garden pretending to look at things. Mum gives me a concerned glance. I know I am acting a bit simple, but I can't sit there any longer with Ally. I wander around for ages, not that there is much to look at in Auntie Jess's garden. The rose bushes have been pruned so hard they have just one perfect flower.

During our picnic Ally talks about gardening to Gramps. She seems sickeningly knowledgeable and discusses the Chelsea Flower Show and decking with him. Gramps seems really entertained by her as she rattles on about herbaceous borders and vegetable plots and the best time to plant garlic. It makes me really jealous. He's my Gramps, not hers, and I want to talk to him. I wish I'd taken more interest in gardening over the years.

Ally asks if he watches the gardening programme that's on every afternoon. '*The Gardener's Diary* is really good,' she says. 'I never miss it.' She checks her watch. 'It's on in ten minutes. We must go inside and watch it. You'll really enjoy it.'

She goes on and on about the programme. So eventually Mum ties Mabel up, we take our shoes off, and make our way into Auntie Jess's immaculate sitting room to watch the TV.

'I'll make us some coffee,' Mum says.

Gramps settles himself down in an armchair. 'Well, this will make a nice change,' he says.

I curl up on the settee. I am pretty tired—if I put my head down on one of Auntie Jess's soft, white lace cushions I could easily fall asleep. But even through this fog of weariness I am aware of Ally being strange. She doesn't sit down but walks around the room talking all the time. She seems really tense. And she's not taking any notice of me—instead her watchful rodent eyes never leave Gramps's face.

Thankfully, as soon as the programme starts, she shuts up. She sits down on the floor beside Gramps's chair like a watchful wolf keeping an eye on its prey. Like me, Gramps is looking pretty sleepy. He may well nod off during the programme because he's not a great fan of television. But as soon as the presenter appears on the screen Gramps sits up and takes notice.

He's wide awake now. 'Good Lord, what a surprise!' he says.

For a second I glimpse a gleeful expression on Ally's face. But then I turn back to Gramps. I am intrigued to find out what has startled him so much. 'What is it?' I ask.

'See that lass, there,' he says to me, pointing to the presenter. 'I know her.'

'Do you really?' I say, impressed. 'Is she one of your customers?'

'No, she was like one of our family. She was engaged to your dad—they were at school and college together. She got interested in gardening because of Rob. She's done well for herself, hasn't she?' he adds with satisfaction. 'She's a grand lass. I bet she's quite a pin-up down the allotments.'

Ally bursts out laughing at that. But I don't bother to look at her. I am too busy staring at the woman on the screen. She has short, dark, curly hair and a square country-woman's face with ruddy cheeks. There is something vaguely, disturbingly, familiar about her. And I wonder if I have seen a photograph of her at some time and forgotten about it until now. She's wearing jeans, a checked shirt, and wellingtons, and yet still manages to look surprisingly trendy.

Somewhere in the back of my memory I recall hearing something about Dad being engaged to someone before Mum—but now the woman is in front of me I am much more interested.

'Yes,' Gramps continues. 'That's Polly Marshall, as

was. I imagine she's married by now. She was a bit on the wild side, but none the worse for it. It's a treat to see her.'

'You liked her a lot, didn't you?' Ally says to him.

'Yes,' Gramps says, smiling. 'She was like one of our own bairns. My wife, Jean, was like a second mother to the girl.'

Mum comes into the room with the coffee pot. She's looking anxious. I expect she's worried about me and coffee anywhere near Auntie Jess's cream carpet. 'Did you know Dad was engaged to her?' I ask Mum, pointing at the TV screen.

'Oh yes, that's Polly, isn't it? Your dad told me she was on TV now. I met her only once years ago—she still looks just the same, which is reassuring,' Mum says, smiling.

'Don't you mind—that Dad was engaged to someone before you?' I ask her.

'No.' Mum sounds surprised. 'Why should I mind?'

'I don't know,' I mumble. My emotions are on fire—I can't believe that Mum can be so cool about something so important.

'Your dad and Polly went out together for years— all through their school days. It was a real teenage love affair,' Mum says, with an indulgent smile. 'They planned a huge family with sons and daughters named after the characters from their favourite books. They wanted to go to New Zealand and start a market garden, but it all fizzled out.'

'Fizzled out?' I echo, astonished. 'How is that

130

possible? How can that happen?' I say. I don't care about Dad and Polly. I am thinking about Spence. Surely how I feel about him will never fizzle out and go flat like a bottle of pop that has been left open?

Gramps laughs. 'I think our Alice is smitten. Who is the lucky lad?' he asks. I am aware of Ally staring at me with a curious, eager look. Maybe she thinks I am going to go into confessional mode and blurt out the details of my love life. But Mum smiles at me sympathetically—almost as if she knows the thoughts that have been going through my mind.

'I thought the first boy I fell in love with was "the one"—until I met your father,' she says gently.

I want to steer the conversation well away from myself, so I ask quickly: 'But that woman—Polly—she must have minded shed-loads when Dad chucked her for you.'

'I don't think there was any chucking. These things just happen,' Mum says casually. She starts to hand around the cups of coffee. I put mine down on a coaster and stare at the woman on the screen. If things had worked out differently she might have been my mother. And I could be living in New Zealand. It's a seriously weird feeling. And, as *Alice in Wonderland* is Dad's fave book, I might still be called Alice . . .

Chapter 13

I don't get the chance to talk to Sam until he arrives early in the morning. I am so pleased to see him I fling my arms around him and give him a hug.

'I've got so much to tell you,' I gabble, as I grab hold of his hand and drag him into the workshop.

'My phone is bust. I did try to ring you, honest,' he says breathlessly. 'Tell me what's been going on. Has Ally, your stalker, been here?'

'Yes! She has!' I say excitedly. I tell him what has been happening: how Ally is pursuing Ed (although he seems to enjoy it), and how she stayed the night—and zonked everyone out with Calvados—so she could rove around the house prying into all the cupboards. And then finally how she invited herself along to visit Gramps.

'Incredible though it seems, she acts as if she wants *everyone* in the family to love her. She made such a fuss of Gramps—greasing up to him like mad. It was unreal. Why is she so obsessed with all of us?'

'I think there's more to it than that,' Sam says slowly. He is frowning with concentration. 'She's being nice to everyone because she wants access to your home. Your family must have something of value that she's after. Think hard, Alice. Did your gran have any really amazing jewellery? Or does your gramps have a priceless painting? Something valuable she could have heard about and wants to steal?'

I stare at him in amazement and then shake my head. 'Our family isn't into stuff like that. Honestly, we have hardly any money or valuables of any kind. Our house in town has an enormous mortgage on it. Gramps owns the garden centre and the land where he grows things. I suppose all that must be worth quite a bit—but if he sold the garden centre he'd have nowhere to live.'

'She must be looking for something. There must be some kind of clue to what it is,' Sam says. 'Next time she comes here you must watch her all the time. She's bound to show her hand eventually.'

'She won't be coming back for a couple of weeks, thank goodness—she's going away to America any day now.' I watch his face for any sign of disappointment. I am worried that he has offered to come to help me because he's intrigued by the mystery of Ally. Everyone else in the world seems to be fascinated by her. Maybe Sam is too.

'Phew! A couple of weeks without her ever-watchful presence—that'll be a relief for you,' he says, smiling at me. 'You're really fed up with her, aren't you?'

'Yes,' I admit. 'It seems like an overreaction but I really hate the feeling that she's watching us and following me around. And not knowing why is the hardest part. Do you think maybe she's just very nosy and a bit bonkers?' I ask. 'She could have an obsession with other people's junk. She might have been banned from every charity shop and jumble sale in the country.'

Sam laughs and shakes his head. 'It's a neat idea, Alice. And it would make a great film, wouldn't it? But,' he adds regretfully, 'I do think there's more to it than that. And I think she'll be back. So next time she turns up ring me straight away. I'll give you my home number and my mum's mobile so you can always get hold of me. I'm sorry I wasn't around when you needed me.'

I am a bit embarrassed when he says that. He seems to know how completely desperate I've been to talk to him. I've an uncomfortable feeling that I may have left some very needy messages on his mobile. To cover my confusion I show him around the greenhouses and the shop.

'What we really want,' I say with a sigh, 'are some more customers—preferably a coach-load of old ladies who will buy all these plants. If they're not sold by the winter they'll be wasted. But everyone goes to the new superstore on the main road now. It may be called Garden Heaven but it's been hell on earth for Gramps. It's ruined his business and even Gary, who's worked for Gramps since he left school, has jumped ship—like a greedy rat—and got himself a job there.'

'Hey! I've got a great plan! Why don't we have a

half-price sale and try to get rid of all the stock?' Sam suggests. 'We could make a big sign and put it up at the crossroads and divert all the superstore's customers. We could put: "The cheapest plants in Yorkshire— everything half price." All the punters love a bargain.'

'Did anyone ever tell you that you're a genius,' I say, because I am genuinely struck by the brilliance of his plan. I think of how great it will be to have the till full of notes and cheques and for Gramps to have some money going into the bank.

'Do you think we ought to ask your gramps first?' he says.

'Yes. I'll text him. But I won't tell the others. I'll let it be a surprise.'

It will be easy enough not to tell anyone what we are doing. Dad is out working every minute of the day—Mum says he's taken on far too many jobs. Nell and Ed come home only to pick up clean clothes and sleep. And even Mum dashed out of the house first thing this morning because she's started a college course for executives who need to retrain.

Gramps is fine about the sale. So Sam (who has wonderful handwriting) gets out the marker board used for orders and writes a huge sign. Then we carry it up to the main road together.

I make us a sandwich and get some cold drinks organized as we wait for customers. 'Do you think it will be like the January sales?' I ask jokingly. 'We might end up with a queue going right across the yard and out the gate,' I add with a laugh.

The oddest thing happens. We really are busy! It isn't quite like the January sales but it is very satisfactory; first a little trickle and then a steady stream.

'This is amazing!' I say to Sam. 'I had no idea we would get so many people.'

'It is pretty incredible, isn't it?' he says grinning.

Then we find out why so many customers have arrived to buy from us. 'It's lucky for you that the Garden Heaven store on the main road is closed,' a kindly-faced woman says to us.

'Closed?' I say, puzzled. 'But it's open seven days a week—eight till late.'

'Well, there's a big sign outside saying it's closed until further notice. Even the car park is shut off so you can't get into the café. I was most disappointed. I promised my kids an ice cream and a drink.' She looks down at the two little children hanging on to her hands and smiles ruefully.

'Oh dear,' I say. 'I'm sorry, we don't sell anything like that.'

'It's an ill wind and all that,' she adds. 'Garden Heaven being shut has done you a bit of good. Everyone is coming down here.'

'Yes, we have been very busy. We thought it was our half-price sale,' I say.

I think no more about it until Gary slinks in. He is still wearing his beanie hat, but, as a concession to the blistering heat, is kitted out in a faded *Kiss* T-shirt and pair of grubby cut-off denims.

'I suppose you've heard,' he says, giving me a wink.

I wipe the perspiration from my forehead with the back of my hand and stare across at him, trying hard not to frown. I hate being winked at. 'Heard about what?' I ask politely. Gramps has always said Gary isn't the brightest spark in the bonfire and it pays to be patient with him.

'The news about them up the road . . .' Gary says, grinning at me. He gestures with his thumb in the direction of the main road.

'The Garden Heaven superstore—our biggest rival until today—is that what you are talking about?' I ask politely. 'We know they are shut,' I add.

'Yep. They've been nobbled good and proper. Wasn't you that did it, was it?' he says, with a sly look.

'Nobbled? What on earth are you talking about? And why should it be anything to do with me?' My voice must have risen sharply because Sam finishes serving his customer and comes over to us.

'What's up?' he asks.

'He says the superstore has been nobbled,' I say quietly. 'Explain, please, Gary.'

Gary giggles. 'Someone put weedkiller—gallons of it and extra strength—into the irrigation system. Everything is dying down there.'

'When did this happen?' Sam asks.

'Last night. The CCTV picked up on someone inside—got in with some wire cutters—went straight to the water tank. Looks like a professional job, according to reports. Someone wanted to put them out of business. As soon as the early shift got in they could see summat was up. Every blinking plant in the place was drooping and turning brown. They did a test on the water and found out they'd been nobbled.' He taps his nose and adds, 'Hope you've got a good alibi for last night, Alice.'

'Why the hell should it be anything to do with Alice?' Sam says furiously. His face is grim and Gary takes a step backwards.

'I never said it was Alice,' he whines. 'Just that word is out that the person they caught on the CCTV was likely as not a girl. Looks bad now, don't it, you raking in the money here. When everyone knows the superstore has pretty well closed the old fella down and it's the end of the line for him.'

'Don't you dare call my gramps an old fella in that rude way,' I say crossly. 'And he's not at the end of anything!'

'Sorry,' Gary says mockingly. 'Anyway, I thought I'd warn you that Mr Lambert, the manager, is on his way down here to see you. He's in a right old rage. So you better have your story ready.'

'I don't need a bloody story,' I snap. 'I didn't go anywhere near the garden centre last night.'

'All right, all right, keep your hair on,' Gary mutters, as he slinks off.

For a long moment Sam and I stand and stare at each other. I shake my head. 'I was at home with Mum, then, when Dad came home, I took Mabel for a walk to the river. I stayed there for ages . . . Oh my goodness, Sam. I don't have an alibi, do I? I was wandering around on my own.'

I am trying hard not to panic but my voice is shrill, and nervous sweat is trickling down my forehead and making my hands clammy.

'Hey, just calm down,' Sam says, putting his hands on my shoulders and looking into my face. 'Get real, Alice. They can't just accuse you of something like this out of the blue. And if they do try to set you up I won't let them. I'll ring my dad. My uncle is a barrister. I'll get his email and fax number. You're not in this alone.'

'My parents will be so upset if people start saying I did something like that . . .' I begin to say, blinking back tears.

More customers arrive. I wipe my eyes and try to concentrate on serving them. But all the time worries are whirling around in my head. Gary is right—it does look bad. And the sale—which seemed such a wonderful idea—is really bad timing. It's as if we knew the superstore would be out of action and are cashing in on their disaster.

At the end of the afternoon, when we have put up the closed sign and brought the board back from the main road, a van with a Garden Heaven logo pulls into the yard. I know that the threatened visit is about to take place. At least we've had a bit of warning.

Mr Lambert is quite young with very short blond hair and anxious blue eyes. He looks mega stressed.

He frowns at us both as if sizing us up. 'I suppose you've heard the news,' he says.

'Gary Barrett was here,' I say. 'He told us about it.'

'It's a bad business. You've not had any problems, have you?' His eyes dart around the greenhouses where everything is crisp and colourful and well watered. 'Obviously not,' he adds. 'Would you just mind telling me exactly how tall you are?' he suddenly says to me.

Sam shakes his head at me, but I answer automatically. 'Five two,' I say.

'Would you mind coming to this side of the counter so I can check that?' Mr Lambert asks, his voice resigned and rather weary.

'Hang on a minute. How about telling us why you are asking this?' Sam says firmly. 'Alice isn't doing anything or answering any of your questions until you've explained yourself.'

'It doesn't really matter,' Mr Lambert says. 'I just want to be a hundred per cent certain there isn't the slightest chance of it being her on the CCTV film that we have of the saboteur.'

'It's OK, Sam,' I say. 'I've got nothing to hide.' I walk around to Mr Lambert's side of the counter and stand next to him. He looks down at me and gives a rueful kind of smile.

'Sorry to put you through this. We have a good silhouette of the culprit next to a door so we can gauge exactly how tall she is. She's my height. That's all we've got to go on at the moment. She was well muffled up. It must be someone who has got a grudge against us. It was all so well planned. It's ruined most of our stock and the whole sprinkler system is contaminated.'

'That doesn't mean you can jump to conclusions about people who just happen to be in the same business as yourself,' Sam says angrily. 'You've no right to come down here and insult Alice like this. It could easily be someone you've sacked or had an argument with in the past.'

'Yes,' Mr Lambert says. 'It was just Gary mentioned . . .'

'Gary's a chuffing half-wit,' Sam says icily. 'Only a lame-brain would take any notice of what he says.'

Mr Lambert edges away from Sam and looks uncomfortable. 'I am very sorry,' Mr Lambert says to me. 'I just wanted to rule out any kind of prank. We are looking into the records to see if there's a past employee who might have a reason to do something like this.'

'It's all right. I don't mind. I am sorry you've lost everything,' I say. I don't like to think of all their plants dying—even though it has done Gramps some good. 'And your apology is accepted,' I add graciously. I am so relieved I can't help smiling. But Sam is still scowling.

'I won't hold you up any more. Good luck with your sale,' Mr Lambert says, as he gets back into his van.

Neither of us speaks until the van has disappeared. Then Sam turns to face me. 'Well—this is a bit of a turn up. I wonder if we should check out the crag sometime soon?' he asks.

'Do you really think she might be up there?' I ask nervously. It's a nasty sensation—the feeling that she might be spying on us. 'Surely she's got better things to do than watch us work. She must have packing to do if she's going to America . . .' My voice trails off. I want to spin on my heel and look up to the dark stones. I want to check whether there is a shadow or a movement up there that would give her away. But, at the same time, I am too scared to do it.

'Look, it's OK, Alice,' Sam says reassuringly. 'I don't think for a moment that she's up there now. But I'd like to go up to see if there is any sign that she's been there recently.'

'You think it was her who was the saboteur at Garden Heaven, don't you?'

'Yes, don't you?'

I nod my head. 'Although I can't think of any sensible reason why she should do it—apart from the fact that she seemed to really adore Gramps and we were all moaning about the superstore and she got all intense about it. But even if she thought she was helping him it's a gross thing to do. Do you think we should ask to see the CCTV and try to ID her?'

Sam shakes his head. 'I don't really see that we have much to give them even if we could ID her—which I very much doubt. A silhouette isn't much to go on. We don't know her surname or where she lives. For all we know she isn't even called Alice. Do you know the full registration number of her car?'

'No,' I say.

'We could tell them there's been an odd girl hanging around but it all sounds pretty crap. Also it exposes you and your gramps to suspicion. I think it's best to leave it. But be very careful of her the next time she comes calling. Ring me straight away,' Sam says. 'If she's prepared to do something like that, I just wonder what else she's capable of.'

I think about Ally prowling around the house at night while we all slept. I think about her up on the crag watching us. And a shudder of fear starts in my stomach and spreads all around my body like a sickness. 'Well, if she really is going away to America I'll be safe for two weeks,' I say, trying to sound cheerful and failing miserably.

Sam gives me a sympathetic look as he reaches over and takes hold of my hand. Just at that moment Mum arrives back and waves to us. Sam lets go of my hand.

'I'll get off home,' he says.

I hold my breath. What will I do if Sam only meant to come and help me for one day? How will I manage without him?

'Have a drink before you go,' I say, handing him a bottle of water. He drinks it straight off. His T-shirt is dark with sweat and his face is glowing. We've both worked incredibly hard. I can't believe that he will offer to do more.

'Thanks for all your help today. I couldn't have done it without you,' I say. 'And thanks for sticking up for me with Mr Lambert. I appreciate it.'

He grins and says, 'That's what friends are for. I'll see you in the morning.'

'Are you sure?' I ask, trying to hide my pleasure.

'Course. I'll come and help you until everything is sold. I told you—we're mates, we stick together.'

'Yes,' I say. And then I add in a rush, 'It's been brilliant having you here. I am sick of talking to Mabel. Nell and Ed spend all their time at Spence's house when they're not working. He lives quite close to the supermarket, you see.'

'So you don't see much of him?' Sam asks.

'No. He was here the night Ally came to stay, and that was the first time I'd seen him for ages. Which is a good thing, I suppose,' I add, trying to sound upbeat and positive.

Sam sighs and says, 'You will get over it in time. I promise you. It's just a question of how long it takes. I forced myself to stop thinking about Elmira after she'd made such a bloody fool of me. But it wasn't easy. And the worst thing was, I couldn't even talk to Lal, my best mate, about it. He was busy writing love letters to her and telling me what a fantastic little sex-pot she was. As if I needed or wanted to know all that.' He laughs drily.

'Do you still think about her?' I ask curiously,

because I can't imagine a time when I won't think about Spence.

'Sometimes,' he admits. 'When I need reminding not to make a prat of myself over some woman who doesn't give a stuff about me . . .' He laughs to take any sting out of those words. But I know suddenly, and with certainty, that he will never try to kiss me again or ask me out, or anything like that. From now on we will just be friends. I ought to be pleased. It's what I wanted after all. But I'm not—which is very puzzling.

Chapter 14

When I wake up the next morning I am happy. When Ed got home from work last night he reported that he and Ally had called in to see Gramps and then had gone on to the airport together. He watched until her plane took off! She really has gone!

This growing friendship between Ed and Ally is very, very, worrying. And the fact that she wanted to go to see Gramps again is really suspicious. Did she want to gauge his reaction to the sabotage of Garden Heaven? What's it all about? I don't know. One thing for sure—she appears to be a very bad enemy. I wish I'd never got on the wrong side of her.

I have worry overload to the point that I can't be bothered to think about it any more. I am too relieved that Ally really has gone to America! It is such a relief to know that she isn't watching me from the crag and she won't arrive unannounced at the house like a poltergeist.

And, what is even better, Sam is coming over every single day to help me sell Gramps's plants. Looking after the garden centre had seemed like a penance, but now suddenly it seems like fun.

Because I am happy the days fly by. Admittedly,

sometimes working in the greenhouses does bear a close resemblance to torture because of the heat. We take it in turns to go in there to do the watering. Unbelievably the weather gets even hotter—it regularly touches 30 degrees—but we don't care. We have loads of laughs and water fights and a really good time. Sam is a great companion. He has the most amazing patter with the customers. Sometimes he makes me laugh so much I have to disappear into the workshop and giggle on my own. But it certainly works. We make masses of money—and even though we make a small fortune Sam won't take a penny in wages.

I keep Gramps posted on how well the sale is going, but it's secret from everyone else. I tell myself what fun it will be to surprise them all. And thinking about the look on Nell's and Ed's faces when they find out how much money we've made always makes me smile.

It comes as quite a shock when the very last customer leaves and I look along the empty shelves. And suddenly all my happiness seems to melt away. I tell myself it's because the empty greenhouses are a very sad sight. By rights they should be full of autumn and winter stock—but there is nothing, because no one has done any planting.

But, if I am honest, the real reason I feel so miserable is because there is no reason for Sam to come over any more. Why have I been such a fool? We've been talking, planning, thinking about selling everything—counting down to the very last trans-action. And now it's happened it doesn't seem like any kind of reason for celebrating. In fact it means there's going to be a big empty hole in my life.

'Thanks for all your help,' I say to him, trying hard to sound cheerful.

'Now ring me when Ally, the stalker, arrives, won't you? I think she will come back eventually,' he adds.

He seems pretty miserable. We stare at each other unsmilingly. It's been nearly three weeks since Ally went away and there has been no sign of her. I'd always thought if she disappeared for good I would celebrate for a year—but now I'm not so sure. At least if she turns up it will give me an excuse to ring Sam.

'Yes, course. I'll phone you right away,' I say.

'See you soon then, Alice,' he says to me, as he gets on his bike.

'Yes, I hope so,' I say, as I wave him off. But when will I see him? I don't know. It's really depressing.

I am moping in front of the TV when Mum phones and says she will be late and can I organize some supper. I make lots of salad and open tins of tuna and get garlic bread out of the freezer.

Then I hang around and wait for everyone to arrive. I try to talk myself into a good mood by telling myself I should be excited and happy. Tonight I am going to give them all a real shock when I tell them I've sold all the old stock and Gramps's cash box is stuffed full of money. For one of the few times in my life

I've done something amazing—something that is bound to impress Nell and Ed.

Mum comes home and tells me I'm a star for getting the supper sorted out. She looks really tired and her hair needs cutting. The worst thing is she smells strongly of extra-strong mints and perfume—which tells me straight away that she is still smoking. I imagine her standing outside the college with all the dead beats, busily lighting one cigarette from the stub of another. It's a horrible image. I wish I could think of something I could say to make her stop.

'How was your course? Are you enjoying it? Do you think it will help you get a job?' I ask her. Maybe if she got a job she really liked she would kick the cigs for good.

Mum shakes her head: 'The course is fairly terrible. And I don't imagine it will help me to get a job. The world seems to be full of redundant executives and middle-aged women with the wrong qualifications—and I am one of them. It's been purgatory today. The college is so hot: there's too much glass and not nearly enough windows that open.'

It is on the tip of my tongue to say that smoking foul-smelling cigarettes that block her arteries and clog her lungs must make her feel even hotter. But I bite back the words.

I think of the years that she nagged me about biting my nails: the awful-tasting stuff she painted on them, the emotional blackmail she used. It didn't do any good. I stopped only when Hannah and Chloe started secondary school with me. They were both into nail varnish in a big way. I found doing my nails extremely boring, but I didn't want to be left out. And I stopped nibbling at mine because painting mutilated little stumps was really humiliating.

I talk about how hot it has been. It's a good neutral subject. 'Do you think the weather will break soon?' I say. 'Even Mabel is feeling the heat. She wouldn't go in the river today. She just paddled a bit and then sat on the bank and panted as if she was an old lady.'

'She is piling on the pounds,' Mum says, looking down at Mabel who is standing by the kitchen table watching my every move. 'When it cools down we must try to give her more exercise. Anyway, I'm going to have a shower before anyone else gets home,' she adds.

I realize that Mabel is showing an unhealthy amount of interest in the tuna so I put it in the fridge and give her a dog biscuit. 'Mum's right. You are getting fat,' I say, looking hard at her. 'Fatty tumkins Mabel—you great porker.'

It is while I am stroking her ears, and she is looking up at me adoringly, that the thought comes into my mind. The terrible, ghastly, awful thought—that Mabel might be pregnant. And that is the reason she has got so fat.

I count up the weeks since the party. Nearly five weeks. I remember Gramps telling me that dogs are pregnant for nine weeks and each week is the equivalent of a month in a human pregnancy. So if Mabel was a woman she would be nearly five months gone. And she looks it. I can see the curve of her belly, a definite droop. Pups—lots of them.

The tears come immediately. I sit on the floor next to her and sob into her collar. She seems bemused and licks my face. I am gutted. I thought that everyone would be so pleased with me because of the plant sale. But now this! They will all be thinking, 'Give Alice a job and she cocks up'—and it's true. I have tried so hard to look after Mabel but I've made a complete hash of it.

The more I look at Mabel the more I know the truth. She is expecting pups. Not lovely pedigree puppies that would sell for hundreds of pounds and make Gramps some extra cash. No, these will be bastard pups, sired by a grotty old sheepdog, difficult to find homes for, just a complete nuisance and something else for Gramps to worry about.

'Mabel! How could you do this to me?' I say. But I know even as I utter these words that I am being unfair. Mabel was following her instincts—doing what comes naturally. It is me who is at fault, I didn't look after her well enough.

Spence arrives with Nell and Ed which should make me feel better but doesn't. It actually makes me so nervous that my hands begin to shake. I am acutely aware of the fact that my eyes and nose are red from weeping and I look like a freak. But it's not just that. I also realize that slowly over the last few weeks Spence has drifted into the back of my mind. I've had other things to think about. But seeing him reawakens all the old longings and feelings and I begin to hurt all over again.

Dad thanks me for getting supper ready, then he says grace, and we pass the food around. I look down at the salad and tuna on my plate. There is a huge lump in my throat and guilt and misery have driven away my appetite. Wasting food is not an option in our house. Dad works too hard to put it on the table. I know now is the time to 'fess up about Mabel.

'I've got some good news and some very bad news,' I say.

'Tell us the good news, Alice,' Mum says kindly, smiling at me.

'I've sold all the plants in the greenhouses. All the summer stock has gone.'

'Well done, sweetheart,' Dad says. 'You must have worked incredibly hard. How did you manage all on your own?'

'I wasn't on my own. Sam came over every day to help me . . .' my voice is squeaky with nerves.

Mum says, 'He seems such a very nice boy—how kind of him to give up his holiday to help you.'

'Yes,' I say, and I take a big drink of water. I am playing for time. Next is the bad news. And I don't know how I am going to tell them.

'This Sam must be sweet on Alice to work in this heat. I think I detect romance in the air,' Nell says laughing. 'He's been hanging around all summer, like an ardent tom-cat.'

Everyone laughs, everyone is happy except me. Spence smiles at me—and makes a joke about how I've kept it a closely guarded secret that I have a boyfriend. But I am too stressed to really take in what he is saying or to reply. I look away quickly.

'There's a problem—I have to tell you the very bad news . . .' I mutter, and I have their full attention then. All eyes are on me. It shreds my nerves and sends my brain haywire.

'Alice, don't look so stricken—what on earth is the matter?' Dad says, in a concerned voice. 'Come on, love. It can't be anything so very terrible, can it?'

'I'm afraid it's an unwanted pregnancy,' I mumble.

Chaos breaks out. Mum gives a little heartbroken cry and clutches her mouth as if she's taken poison. Dad stands up so quickly his chair falls over.

'Oh-my-god-Alice . . .' Nell breathes, and she puts her hand over her eyes as if to block out all sight of me. Spence looks as if his heart is slowing down and Ed's mouth is flapping like a beached fish.

'I'm very sorry . . .' I say. They all stare at me dumbly. 'I did try to keep an eye on her, but she was so naughty about running away . . . Do you think Gramps will ever forgive me?'

'Mabel!' Mum cries, just as if she's won the lottery.

'Thank the Lord,' Dad says quietly, and he picks up his chair and sits down.

The penny drops—I realize what they have all been thinking. My face heats and my eyes fill with sharp tears that trickle down my burning cheeks.

Spence leans over the table and gently rubs his hand across my knuckles. I feel the roughness of his fingertips that comes from playing his guitar. 'Don't cry, Alice,' he says softly. Then he turns to Nell and adds: 'Nelli—I think you'd better tell.'

Nell looks uncomfortable. 'I'm very sorry, Alice,' she says humbly. 'I think maybe I am to blame—not you. You see Spence and I took Mabel down to the river one evening and she got jumped on by a golden retriever. We thought it was another girl to begin with, but then . . .' her voice trails off.

'Why didn't you say something at the time?' I say aghast.

Nell shoots a glance at Spence and then says: 'I suppose . . . we thought . . . we hoped it would be all right.'

'And to think I've always been told I am the dim one in the family,' I say bleakly. 'It's a mercy for the animal kingdom that neither of you is down for veterinary college, isn't it?'

'We thought they were just playing about—we weren't watching that carefully,' Nell says sheepishly. And then the most extraordinary thing happens. She blushes. I don't think I have ever seen her scarlet with embarrassment before. I thought I was the only one in the family who suffered the humiliation of colouring up when upset.

'I suppose it might have been the collie from the farm,' I say with an attempt at fairness. 'Mabel did get away from me at the crag on the day of the party.'

'Well, we'll soon know when the puppies arrive, won't we?' Mum says.

'How long before they are born?' Ed asks.

'About four weeks,' I say.

'They'll be an awful lot of work,' Dad warns.

'I don't mind,' I say. 'I'll do it all, I promise.'

'Well, you must make sure that you don't get behind with your school work. Dad and I are very keen for you to do well,' Mum says. 'How have you got on with your history?'

It seems that all eyes are on me again. I stare down at my salad and push it from one side of the plate to the other. 'I've made loads of notes,' I mutter. 'I just need to type it all out.'

'Well, we can close the shop now,' Dad says reassuringly. 'And then you can get on with your school work in peace. Have you had any luck with getting our computer fixed?' he asks Ed and Nell.

'No. It's too old,' Nell says. 'It's just about ready for a museum. But it doesn't matter. Ally's back from America and she has given me her spare laptop for Alice to use. She's left it round at Spence's house. I'll bring it back and put it in my room—there's more space for you to work in there,' Nell says bossily to me.

I sit mute and miserable. Ally is back. She is friends again with Ed and Nell. She's been round to Spence's house. It's as if she is part of their gang. And because of that she has managed to get her own way and meddle in my life. Maybe . . . frighteningly . . . she always gets what she wants eventually. She wanted me to use the laptop and now I have to. I feel her presence in the room like the chill draught of air. And even though the evening is as warm as a tropical night a sudden shiver runs down my back. It's as if she is here in the house again, insinuating herself into our lives like a dark shadow.

'I don't think I know how to use a laptop,' I mumble tearfully.

'It's a breeze. And it's got an internet connection. Why don't you surf the net for some good photos?' Ed suggests. 'We always got top marks for illustrated work. I'll have a look with you if you like,' he adds kindly.

'OK,' I mutter reluctantly. I don't know why my bloody course-work has suddenly become so important to everyone. It seems as if the whole happiness of the household rests on my history project. And this is more bad news.

A new tremor of apprehension runs through me. My history notes are chaotic. I've spent too much time working in the shop and having a laugh with Sam. When I have worked on my history I've been on automatic pilot. I will have to read it through and see if it makes any kind of sense at all. I sigh and feel sorry for myself—because now my project has become something else to worry about. Troubles seem to be chasing me like a pack of mad dogs. And the maddest dog of all is Ally. I wish she hadn't come back.

Chapter 15

I arrange to meet Sam in town. I have some news that is too incredible to discuss over the phone (anyway I want to see him). I force myself not to blab it as soon as I see him—which is really hard. I'm quite proud of myself because I manage to wait until we are in the park and Sam has bought us both an ice cream from the kiosk.

We sit down on a bench. 'I don't know where to start,' I say. 'The most extraordinary things have been happening!'

'Start at the beginning,' he suggests, with a grin.

'Well, you're not going to believe it. Our house in Bradley Road is rented out. And the tenants phoned Mum and were uppity. They said if we wanted to go into the house and take stuff out of the attic we should ask them and arrange a time—not just go into the house when they weren't there.'

There is a stunned silence from Sam and then he whistles. 'That can't just be a coincidence, Alice!' he says. 'It must be her. Who else has an abnormal interest in attics and junk that belongs to your family?'

I nod excitedly. 'Evidently the tenants got home, and they are mega house-proud, and they noticed immediately that there was a lot of dust on the landing. And then, when they looked up at the trap that leads into the loft, they could see a dirty handprint. And whoever had been in the loft washed their hands and left a ring in the washbasin. These people must have a cleanliness fetish because no one would ever have noticed stuff like when we lived there.

'Anyway,' I continue. (I am enjoying having his attention.) 'There was no sign of a break-in. So Mum got all twitchy about keys and Ed confessed that he had lost his keyring and the back-door key for Bradley Road was on it. And Ally is back from America and spending a lot of time with Ed and Nell—worse luck. She's even given Nell her laptop for me to use. Not that I want anything of hers. I hate her. I wish she'd go away and leave us alone.'

Sam is leaning forward. I can tell he's really excited about what I've told him. 'It must be her—and it's such a completely crazy thing to do. It proves that she's still hunting for something that your family owns. Tell you what—why don't we go to the hotel behind the conference centre and see if she's staying there again?'

'OK, I suppose we could do that,' I say a bit uncertainly. I want to spend time with him but, if I'm honest, I'm not really that keen on tracking Ally down or seeing her again.

'If we find out where she's staying at least we'll know where she's based. We've got so little to go on. She arrives and creates havoc and we never find out any more about her,' Sam says, frowning with concentration. Then he looks into my face and adds quietly: 'Alice, have you got any idea of what she is looking for? Think really hard. It must be something to do with your family, mustn't it?'

I look into his intense blue eyes and say, 'Honestly, Sam, I haven't got a clue.'

'Alice . . .' he says slowly. 'Say it was something bad—something that would upset you. Would you still want to know?'

'What kind of thing?' I ask, bemused.

'I don't know. It could be a skeleton in the family cupboard—something from the past that no one talks about: drink, disgrace, illegitimacy, prison. Most families have something, or someone, they don't discuss. I have a great-uncle Harry who is a forbidden topic. Any mention of him practically gives my grandma a heart-attack.'

'I think I would still want to know,' I say slowly. 'I think I'll risk it. Really I'd just like to solve the mystery of why she is stalking us—and then tell her to get lost.'

'OK,' he says. 'You know I'm always here for you, don't you?'

'Yes,' I say. 'That's what mates are for, isn't it?'

'Sure thing,' he says lightly.

It's a long walk to the conference centre. The pavements are bleached white by the sun and heat reflects off the buildings and is trapped. There isn't a breath of wind and the air is hot and still, and laden with exhaust fumes. I feel sweat trickling down my back.

The hotel is set back from the road and is surrounded by a low red-brick wall. 'Let's have a walk around the car park,' Sam says. I try to get interested—I tell myself we are like undercover cops and it's really exciting. But I can't get up any enthusiasm. I don't know what we'll do if we find Ally's car, anyway. But Sam is obviously enjoying himself, so I wander around with him looking at all the cars. But there is no sign of the pink Beetle.

'She's not here,' I say. 'Maybe we should look at the crag. Or perhaps she's lurking at a car-boot sale or having fun at a flea market,' I add quickly. I wish I'd kept quiet about the crag—the idea of Ally up there watching us always manages to give me the horrors. Sam smiles at me sympathetically.

'Maybe,' he says thoughtfully, 'she's got a different car. Chances are she'd still have her personalized number plate.'

We retrace our steps, looking at all the registration numbers. All the cars are smart and new. There is a very flashy Mercedes jeep. The number plate is PO 11Y.

'I suppose that jeep must belong to someone called Polly . . .' Sam says.

'Yes—someone with more money than sense,' I say dismissively, as I glance into the back of the Mercedes. It's full of gardening equipment. Everything stacked neatly—just the way Dad does it.

The jeep belongs to a gardener. A gardener called . . . Polly . . . POLLY! My mind is racing like a river in flood. I can't keep up with the flow. A gardener called Polly. Surely there must be lots of them . . .

But I remember being at Auntie Jess's house with Gramps and Ally. And the programme Ally insisted we watch. That programme featured a gardener called Polly, a woman who learnt the love of growing things from Dad. A woman who Dad had loved for years and years—a woman he was going to marry until he met Mum. I begin to feel sick and I wish I hadn't had the ice cream. I can feel my stomach doing somersaults.

I go and sit down on the wall that divides the car park from the pavement and sink my head into my hands.

'Alice, are you OK?' Sam asks anxiously. He sits down on the wall and puts his arm around me. 'I'm sorry. Did I walk too fast on the way up here? Do you feel faint?'

I shake my head. 'How did you know?' I whisper to him.

'Know what?' he asks gently.

'Know that it would be something bad—a terrible secret about my family.'

'Alice, don't be crazy.' He has both his arms around me now and is trying to look into my face. 'We haven't found out anything yet. Her car isn't here. She isn't here.'

I look at him bleakly. 'I have found out something. And I think she is here. If you go into the hotel and ask them they will tell you that Polly Marshall, the

161

woman who fronts *The Gardening Diary* on TV, is staying here. I expect her daughter is with her. Her daughter is called Alice. And I think she's my sister . . . well, my half-sister.'

'For crying out loud,' Sam says in amazement.

'Dad was engaged to Polly Marshall before he met my mum. He was going to have lots of kids with her—all named after characters in their favourite books.' My chin wobbles—but I just manage to finish what I have to say: '*Alice in Wonderland* is my dad's favourite book.' I chew at my lip. 'I wonder if he has any idea that he has two daughters called Alice,' I say brokenly.

'Shut up, Alice,' Sam says firmly. 'Look, if your dad knew he had another daughter he wouldn't have kept it a secret, surely. I mean there's nothing wrong in it, is there? Lots of people have two families. My uncle has been married twice and now he's got a baby with his girlfriend. I've got three lots of cousins all with different mums. It's not a big deal. It can't be that. Anyway, if Ally suspects that your dad is her dad, what is she looking for in the attic? It must be something else.'

Just as he starts to give me a hug we are interrupted by a gruff voice. 'You can cut that out for a start! This is a private car park. So, clear off and go and rest your butts somewhere else. I've been watching you two. If I catch you snooping around here again I'll call the police.' It's a burly man wearing overalls. He's frowning hard and full of spite.

'We want an autograph, that's all,' Sam says

politely. 'Polly Marshall, the gardener from the TV, is staying here, isn't she? She's my gran's favourite on the box. She'd love a signed photo or something like that.'

'Pull the other one,' the man says rudely. 'Miss Marshall doesn't want to be bothered with the likes of you. And it's none of your business who is staying here. Clear off—before I call the police.'

'And what exactly is it that we have done? Just so you can report the crime correctly,' Sam says with mock politeness. 'Now, let me see. We have walked around your car park and sat on your wall.'

'It's private property,' the man blusters.

'Of course it is—that's why it's a hotel. You might find you are accused of wasting police time. But do go ahead and ring,' Sam says.

I get up off the wall and grab his arm. 'Come on,' I say, and we walk away.

The man shouts abuse at us until we are out of sight. 'What a chuffing gorilla,' Sam says. 'But we found out what we need to know. Polly Marshall is staying there.'

We stare at each other. 'I'm sorry, Alice. It looks as if you might be right,' he says, and puts his arms around me and holds me tight.

I am in such a daze that the next couple of hours are a blur. I know Sam holds my hand and guides me back to town. He takes me to a café and makes me drink hot sweet tea. A long time ago, in what seems like another lifetime, Spence did the same.

I talk to him in garbled sentences. Telling him about Ally making us watch the gardening programme—about how she looked at Dad when he said grace the first time—Gramps always says grace and maybe she'd been told that.

'Everyone loves her—even Gramps. And she'd do anything for him. Even sabotaging the superstore in revenge for what they've done to him. It all makes sense now, doesn't it? She did it because she knows that he's her gramps.'

Sam nods silently.

'And Ed and Nell can't get enough of her,' I continue bitterly. 'It won't be a big deal for them if she's their half-sister. Ed thinks she's the greatest thing since sliced bread. I expect he'd much rather have her for a sister than me.' Then a new and more terrible thought hits me. 'But say my mum doesn't know anything about it? Maybe my dad's never told her. She might go completely mental if she finds out.'

There's nothing he can do to take away the fear and pain. But he hugs me before he puts me on the bus. 'Just ring me any time—day or night. And if you need me I'll come straight away.' I am so choked up I can't even say thank you. Sam has to pay my bus fare because I can't speak to the driver.

The bus journey gives me a chance to pull myself together which is just as well because as soon as I get home Hannah phones me. I can tell straight away that she is crying. My own eyes fill at the sound of her sobbing.

'What is it?' I ask, sniffing hard. 'Don't cry, Han, please.'

'Alfie and Greg have been away surfing in Newquay and me and Clo have just found out they cheated on us while they were there,' she wails.

'Maybe it was just a holiday romance and didn't mean anything?' I say. I am having trouble getting my head around this. I am scared that my family's life is just about to crumble—so being two-timed by your boyfriend really doesn't seem that important. Although I am sorry she's upset and I make a determined effort to sound sympathetic. 'Maybe it was just one of those stupid lad things . . . You know what they're like when they get in a gang,' I suggest, although I'm not sure if this makes it better or not.

'I can't forgive him. He lied to me. I'll never trust him again,' she sobs.

I talk to her for ages trying not to think about my own problems. But all the time the words *lies, trust, forgiveness, truth* are colliding in my brain. I've always trusted my dad absolutely—and I know my mum has too; the thought that he might have kept a secret from us all is really frightening. It makes me feel quite sick to think about it.

Finally Hannah calms down and says, 'I hate boys. We had much more fun when it was the three of us hanging out together, didn't we? Me and Clo should have been like you and not bothered with boys. There's no one you want to go out with, is there? Not even that cool-looking Sam?'

She takes my silence as a 'No' and continues, 'I feel really bad about how we've neglected you this holiday. We haven't come to see you once while you've been stuck out there at Ramsgarth working. And you must have had a really crap time. But now we've finished with Alfie and Greg we can go back to how we used to be, can't we?' she asks wistfully.

'Yes, of course we can,' I say consolingly, like a mother soothing a fretful child. But I am not being completely truthful. I'd love to go back to being part of the witches with Han and Clo. But I haven't had a crap time since I stopped seeing them. Hanging out with Sam, and selling all the plants for Gramps, has been the best fun ever. And I think maybe there is someone I want to go out with. Hidden in the back of my mind is a terrible regret for what I gave up when I turned Sam down. But he seems happy for us just to be friends so I will have to settle for that.

I go in search of Mum. She is sitting at the kitchen table doing Dad's accounts. Her hair is tied back and she looks hot and tired. The sight of her brings a lump to my throat. I would like to be a little kid again. Then I could throw myself into her arms and blurt out everything that has happened and ask her to make it better. But I can't do that.

'Where on earth have you been, Alice? I thought you were going to get on with your school work?' she asks me in a really edgy voice.

'Yes, I'm going to get started,' I say guiltily. I feel bad that I have upset her. If the truth about Ally comes out she is going to be gutted. She doesn't need extra hassle from me.

'Do you need any help with it?' Mum asks briskly.

'It's course-work. We have to do it by ourselves.'

'Alice, I want to ask you something and I want you to answer me truthfully,' she says.

I hold my breath. I feel as if all the knowledge I have about Ally is suffocating me. What shall I say if she asks me about her? What can I say?

'If you had a boyfriend, you would talk to me about it, wouldn't you?' she says. She looks really anxious.

I gently exhale my breath and smile at her. I am so relieved. 'Mum, I haven't got a boyfriend,' I say.

'What about Sam? He's spent a lot of time over here with you.' She is giving me a curious, searching look.

'He's just my friend. We were in the youth theatre together.'

'Well, I saw Gramps today. He has sent some money for you to take Sam out to the cinema and for a meal, to say thank you for helping in the shop.'

'That's brilliant of Gramps,' I say gratefully. 'I'll ring and thank him.'

'Gramps said you're always talking about Sam and he thinks you're very fond of him,' Mum says.

I chew at my lip and try to avoid her eyes. I can feel my face getting hot. 'If I was going to have a boyfriend—which I'm not—but if I was . . . then I suppose I would want it to be Sam,' I say.

167

'Gramps seems to know far more than me about what is going on with my family,' Mum says. 'I feel as if I've neglected you all. That I've always put my work first and Dad has not been able to fill the gap.'

'Mum, that's rubbish,' I say. And she looks so heartbroken I rush over to give her a hug. 'Gramps calls me up and chats, that's why he knows so much. But I've always loved you working and coming back at the weekends and telling me all the exciting stuff that is happening and going to Italy and being bilingual.'

This is terrible. For years she has worried about working full-time and being a mother—insisting when she was feeling down that she did neither job properly. She's so insecure. What will happen when she finds out about Ally? It will be the last straw. I am very afraid that my family is going to break into a thousand pieces and nothing will ever be able to put it back together again.

I take a deep breath and start talking. 'We've never felt neglected. Dad has always been around when we needed him—he always comes to concerts and things at school. He even makes time to pick us up at the end of term. And I've always been able to phone you whenever I wanted. Do you remember when I had my DT practical to work out—when I designed that stupid biscuit cutter? And you read me all Grandmamma's recipes over the phone. You've always been here for me—even when you've been away.'

Mum manages a wan smile and I sit on her knee as if I am a little girl and wrap my arms around her neck. I whisper: *'Ti voglio bene. Tu sei la migliore madre del mondo.'* Because I want her to know that I love her and she is the best mother in the world.

'I'll go and start typing my history work now,' I say.

'Yes, go and do it well and make me happy,' Mum says, giving me another hug.

I wish there was some other way of making her happy. I wish I could magic Ally out of our lives. My brain is spinning with schemes to stop Ally from destroying my parent's happiness—but I can't think of anything sensible. I shall have to get Nell to help me. She's the clever one.

But for now I will worry about my history. I go up to my room and spread my course-work out on the bed. It is my major project for this holiday—and at the moment it is a huge pile of junky paper that will take me for ever to type. I have to get it sorted. And then I have got to find some way to deal with Ally. Despite my best intentions I begin to panic.

Chapter 16

I decide to start typing immediately. Nell is in her room, sorting through her clean washing, so she witnesses my fumbling attempts at trying to get into the laptop. Knowing that it belonged to Ally seems to have put a curse on me. My hands are trembling and I can't seem to function at all.

Nell looks up at me irritably as I mumble to myself and clatter about. I really need to talk to someone about Ally—and the storm clouds which are gathering over us. I am finding it impossible to think about anything else.

'What on earth is the matter with you?' Nell snaps.

'I keep losing my place. I can type really fast on an ordinary keyboard but this is so small.' Then I add miserably, 'It's going to take me at least a hundred years to type all this lot.'

'Please don't exaggerate—it sounds so infantile,' she says sighing.

'Sorry,' I mutter. 'Mum and Dad will be really upset if I'm late with this and I get a report card. And when Mum gets stressed she smokes,' I add miserably. 'I hate her smoking. I wish she'd quit for good.'

I wonder bleakly how many cigs Mum will get through if Ally drops the big one on us.

'Oh well, it's Mum's life, isn't it,' Nell says dismissively. 'I spend too much time trying to organize Spence; I'm not going to start nagging my parents as well.' She comes over to me. 'Give it here—let me have a look,' she says, as she takes hold of my first page.

'It's my course-work; I have to do it all by myself,' I say, trying to pull the sheet away from her. A rather crumpled corner comes away in my fingers. I am ashamed for her to see how messy it is, full of crossings out and mistakes.

'No wonder you can't read it—it looks like hieroglyphics,' she says with a sigh.

'Thanks so much—that's the nicest thing anyone has said to me for ages,' I say wearily.

'Your teachers should be paid danger money for risking their eyesight deciphering this lot,' she adds, flicking through the rest of the pages.

'Just leave me alone, will you,' I shout crossly, as I try to grab the pages back from her. I feel too stressed to cope with insults. 'Nobody asked you to come and poke your nose in and make horrible remarks. I have enough of it at school without you doing it as well.'

'Don't be silly. I'm trying to help you,' she says, more kindly. 'Look, how about if I read it aloud and you type? I could spell out some of these words you've got wrong at the same time.'

'I don't know . . .' I say uncertainly. I am sulky because she has teased me. But I am desperate to get my course-work out of the way. I also have this superstitious feeling that I have made a bargain with fate—if I do well with my history some miracle will happen and Ally will disappear for good.

'I won't change anything,' Nell says. 'It will still be all your ideas. All I'll do is read it out. It will be quicker.'

'OK,' I say reluctantly.

She stretches herself out on the bed, as gracefully as a Siamese cat, and begins to read. Just occasionally she laughs at my phonetic spelling but most of the time she's very good and goes at the right speed. We get through the pages like magic.

Finally I reach a stage of complete exhaustion and can't type another word.

'We'll do some more tomorrow,' Nell says. 'You know, it is very interesting and surprisingly well written. You've done some good research. It's just your presentation that lets you down. Which books did you use? I'd like to have a look at them.'

I hand her my copy of *Women During the Great War* and to my amazement she leans back on the pillows and starts to read it. I find it incredible that anyone—even someone brainy like Nell—should read a history book just for fun.

'Are you going out with Spence tonight?' I ask. I can't stop a little tug of emotion at the thought of seeing him.

'Oh no! Spence is doing some boring gig. I'm not hanging around listening to his band again. Ed and

I are meeting up with Ally. Then we're all going into town.'

I take a deep breath. This is the moment I have been waiting for. I must tell her the truth about Ally. I must get her on my side.

'Nell, I really need to talk to you about Ally. I've found out loads of bad stuff about her. Please listen. It's very important.'

At first Nell is reluctant to leave my history book. I have to pull it away from her and put it behind my back before she will listen. When I have her attention, I try to tell the story properly. I start at the beginning and work through all the things that have happened, all the evidence that I have.

Nell listens to me in silence. Then, when I have finished, she starts to laugh. 'Wait a minute. I must get Ed in here to listen to all this.' She goes out of the room and then hauls Ed in. He is halfway through shaving, one side of his face is covered in foam and the other is smooth.

He grumbles and tries to pull away from her, but Nell closes the door quickly and says: 'Shut up, Ed, stop squawking and listen to this. Tell him, Alice, just like you told me.'

I start again: the crag and the campsite, the red dress and the party, Gramps's sideboard, the break-in at Bradley Road, and then the gardening programme and Dad's relationship with Polly Marshall.

'Are you seriously suggesting that Ally is Dad's

daughter? That is really sick!' Ed says angrily. 'You're bonkers, Alice!'

'It's wonderful, isn't it?' Nell giggles. 'Where did Mum and Dad get her from? She lives in a little world of her own.'

Ed is wiping the foam off his cheek with his hands. He's in a major stress and his face is dark with temper. 'You've no right to make allegations like this without any foundation. Ally told me herself that she camped at the crag because it's been such a wonderful summer and it saved driving when she'd had a drink. And as for all this bullshit about her looking through the sideboard and going through the bin-bags, you dreamt it—you imbecile. You're just jealous of her. You've got some problem with her having the same name as you, and coming along to our party and fitting in and making friends with everyone.'

'I keep on telling you! I don't know why you won't believe me. She wasn't at the youth theatre. I made it up. Anyway, Sam doesn't remember her either,' I say mulishly.

'I'm not listening to any more of this lunatic talk,' Ed says furiously, and he storms out and slams the door.

Nell looks a bit shaken by his outburst. 'Don't take any notice of him,' she says. 'Ally always makes a real fuss of him. So he feels she's his special friend.'

She looks at me and says briskly, 'Come on, Alice. We'll go down and set the table for supper. Just forget all about it. It's just a big misunderstanding on your part. Ally is a laugh. We really like her. And she's coming here this evening to pick us up—so please don't say any more about this. It's all nonsense, you know.'

I shake my head and go and lock myself in my room. Am I insane? Have I imagined the whole thing? Will I wake up and find that I have dreamt everything that has happened during this summer holiday? Is Ed right and I am suffering from delusions and jealousy because they prefer Ally to me and they are in a chummy gang with her and Spence—a chummy gang that I am totally excluded from. They treat me like a lesser life-form.

I fling myself down on the bed and ring Sam. 'I told Nell and Ed about Ally and they think I'm barking,' I tell him. I don't have the courage to say the word 'jealous'. It hits too close to how I feel.

'Do you want me to come over?' he asks sympathetically.

'Yes, please. Ally's coming here to meet up with Nell and Ed. They're all going out together.'

Inside me a massive pain uncoils at the memory of how Ed sprang to Ally's defence and how sociable he and Nell are towards her. She's more than a friend to them—they already treat her like a sister.

'They think she's marvellous and won't hear a word against her,' I add miserably to Sam.

'I'll get over as quickly as I can,' he says. He believes in me. But everyone else thinks I'm crazy. I am scared that Ed is so angry he will tell everyone what I have said and start on about how I am suffering from delusions. I dread him making a scene and the whole story coming out.

When I get downstairs Mum is getting ready to dish up. The kitchen smells of cooking and Mum has tuned the radio into the classical music station. Everything is very homely and peaceful. I fear it is the calm before the storm.

'We won't wait for Dad,' Mum says regretfully. 'I think he's going to be late again.'

We have just started eating when Mabel begins to bark. Ally's pink Beetle and Dad's Land Rover pull into the yard together. 'Oh good, Dad's here,' Mum says in a pleased voice.

'Ally's here too,' Ed says, sounding equally pleased.

'Great! We can get out early and play pool,' Nell adds. And then they both stare coldly at me, as if to let me know exactly who they prefer out of the two Alices.

'Sorry I'm late. Supper smells good,' Dad says, as he washes his hands in the sink. Mum gives Dad his meal, and then fusses around Ally asking her if she would like some food.

Ally doesn't want to eat, but she joins us at the table with a glass of juice. We sit around in uneasy silence for a while until Nell starts talking about her uni place and where she will live in London.

'When you've moved down, we'll have to meet up,' Ally says to Nell. Ed isn't included in this invitation. He's going to uni in Leeds. He scowls down at his food as if it might bite him.

'Lovely, yes, of course we must meet up,' Nell says with a bright smile. 'You can show me the sights.'

'I'd like to introduce you to my mother,' Ally says very deliberately.

There is a beat of silence—I hold my breath—then she turns to Dad and continues, 'My mother is a gardener—like you.'

Dad is busy eating. He started work at six thirty this morning, he must be famished. 'That's nice,' he says, with a quick smile. Then he goes back to his stew and potatoes.

'She's on the television. Do you watch many gardening programmes?' Ally asks—her voice is very casual.

I feel as if all the air is being squeezed out of my lungs; it's like diving too deep into a swimming pool. The world is moving in slow motion and time seems to have stopped. Ed is staring at Ally with his mouth open and Nell is looking wary. Mum is frowning—as if she is trying to put two and two together and coming up with a problem instead of an answer.

I take a deep breath: 'Your mother is Polly Marshall—the presenter of *The Gardening Diary*, isn't she?' I say it too loudly, I am almost shouting.

Dad looks up—my raised voice and the name Polly Marshall has brought him to attention.

'Polly!' he says startled. 'Is she your mother? What an amazing coincidence. Do you know I met her in town a few months ago and that was the first time I'd seen her in twenty years. She said she was hoping to move back to Yorkshire. She'd just got a new contract she was very excited about. So you're her daughter—and you're friends with our little Alice too . . . well, isn't it a small world.' He smiles broadly.

Mum is looking astonished. 'How extraordinary! We were watching your mother on the television only the other day, weren't we?' Mum says. 'Why on earth didn't you tell us then that you are Polly's daughter? Gramps would have been so thrilled.'

Ally ignores Mum. Instead she turns back to Dad. All eyes are on her. Ed's face has gone blotchy and he is blinking too fast. Nell's mouth is pinched up. These signs tell me they are both upset. I'm upset too. I can feel my heart hammering in my chest. If I was old I would probably have a seizure at this moment and fall off my chair.

Ally's voice is low and sharp. 'My mother cried for a week after she met you,' she says accusingly to Dad. He slowly puts down his knife and fork and faces her.

'I'm sorry if that's so. We had a chat about old times—nothing more.'

'Old times,' Ally sneers. 'When she got home she took out all your letters and read them again and cried. She's kept every single one you ever sent her. It was after that I made up my mind to track you down.'

'She's kept all my letters,' Dad echoes, looking bemused.

'Yes, the letters you wrote to her when you were apart,' Ally says. 'I've read them all so I know what you promised. How you said you would keep all her letters for ever and never forget her. But you haven't kept her letters, have you?'

Dad shakes his head. He seems totally confused. I've never seen him like this before.

'You made her a box in woodwork class and she keeps your letters in it. But she lost the engagement ring you bought her. She was heartbroken. Some scumbag at my party stole it.'

'I'm sorry,' Dad says. He looks and sounds bewildered.

'She always says you are the love of her life and she should have married you.'

Dad is completely fazed by this. He glances desperately at Mum as if begging for help. But Mum is looking as shell-shocked as him—no help there. He turns back to Ally and says carefully, 'I'm sorry if Polly was upset after we met again and if you're upset about it. But it all happened a very long time ago. Polly and I were extremely young, we were very fond of each other, and then we broke up. These things happen, don't they?'

'She would never tell me your surname. I tracked you down after she said you were a landscape gardener and lived up here. I felt you ought to know that you have another daughter—also called Alice.'

179

She looks around at us all. On her face is the strangest expression. She doesn't look happy and she doesn't look scared. She looks exultant. As if she's been waiting for this moment all her life.

'*You are my father*,' she says to Dad, and she draws out each syllable so that her words seem to echo around the room and go on for ever.

No one speaks. No one makes a sound. Even Mabel is absolutely silent. Ally repeats it again slowly and carefully: '*You are my father*.'

I want to put my hands over my ears and shut out her voice. I feel as if her words have got inside my head and are eroding my brain cells like a killer virus. I fear if she keeps on saying '*You are my father*' then, in some terrible way, it will turn out to be true.

I stand up. 'No . . .' I say. Then I repeat it again and again until I am shouting it out in a long scream. 'Noooooooo.' And Mabel, agitated by this raw animal noise, starts to howl as if she fears the world is ending. And I suppose in a way it is . . .

Chapter 17

All hell breaks out. Mum leaps across to me as if I am on fire and smothers me against her, talking quickly in Italian, her words rattling like machine-gun fire. I bury my face against her warm, soft body and manage finally to shut up.

Everyone else is making a dreadful racket. Mabel is barking as if there is a wolf at the door. And Ed and Nell are shouting at Ally—both of them telling her she is a two-faced bitch and other appropriate insults—and drowning each other out.

Ally's eyes are round and shocked. She obviously had no idea that at times of stress our Italian lineage comes to the fore and we explode. Finally there is a lull.

Dad—the only one not to have been making a noise—stands up and an uneasy silence falls. He looks across at Ally and shakes his head. He looks so sombre. It makes me want to cry to see the sadness in his eyes.

'I'm very sorry, but you are completely wrong. I'm not your father. I can give you my word on that.'

Ally glares at him. 'You lied in your letters. You didn't keep her letters like you said you would. I don't believe you. You've airbrushed me out of your life before and you're trying to do it again. You even gave *her* my name.' She casts a dismissive glance in my direction before she adds: '*You are my father!* You have to face it.'

'Why would I want to airbrush you out of my life? Why would I do that if you were my daughter?' Dad says. He looks and sounds upset. 'I was very fond of Polly and we talked about marrying and I bought her a ring. But we were very young and when we spent time apart we both met other people and the whole direction of our lives changed. It was just something that happened. But I never had anything but the fondest of feelings and kind memories of her . . . She was very special to me.'

'But you married someone else! And there was never anyone else for her. There was only ever you!' Ally shouts dramatically.

Dad looks away as if the sight of her hurts his eyes. After a couple of seconds he turns back to her and says slowly, 'You must go and talk to your mother and ask her to tell you the whole story. I'm very sorry if you've been under the impression that I am your father and I didn't want to know about you. Nothing could be further from the truth. If you had been mine and Polly's child I would have loved you, just as I love all my children, and I would have wanted to be part of your life.'

'Will you take a DNA test?' she demands. 'Then we'll know the truth, won't we?' she adds triumphantly. I don't know if she wants him to be her father so she can love him or hate him. I wonder if she knows herself.

'Yes, I'll take a DNA test, if that is the only thing that will satisfy you,' he says slowly. And he rubs his hand across his forehead as if all this talk about the past has given him a headache. Then he pushes his plate of food away as if his appetite has vanished for ever. 'But I suggest you talk to your mother first . . . she has never told you that I am your father, has she?'

Just for a second I see something like anxiety in his eyes and inside my chest I feel a tug of fear. What will I do if Ally is his child? What will I do if she is my half-sister?

'She's never said you're not my father . . .' Ally says with a sly look. 'I wanted to find her letters to see if she wrote and told you about me. Then you couldn't deny it,' she adds defiantly. 'But you haven't kept her letters. I've looked through everything you own and all the stuff your father's kept. I've seen it all: Mother's Day cards made when you were six, your school reports, the books you won at Sunday school, every passport you've ever owned. But no letters! Even though you told her she was the most important thing that ever happened to you and you'd keep them for ever. What did you do with them?' she adds accusingly.

'I really don't remember . . . I suppose they must have gone on a bonfire at some time,' Dad says lamely. He turns to Mum and gives her an anguished look.

Mum sighs, it seems to come from deep within her. I can see that her hands are not quite steady. She'll be dying for a fag . . . 'I think it might be best if you left now, Ally,' Mum says gently. 'There doesn't seem to be much point keeping on raking up the past—especially without Polly here to set the record straight. I think we really need some time on our own to discuss all this. You have to realize that this has been an enormous shock to everyone. Especially for Nell, Ed, and Alice—this is a complete bolt from the blue for them. They thought you were their friend.' There is a definite note of accusation in Mum's voice as she says that.

Ally stands up and looks at Nell and Ed in turn. They refuse to meet her eyes. She doesn't even bother to glance at me. I don't suppose it matters much if I hate her guts. I am the girl who got given her name— poor me. My middle name is Maria. I might insist that everyone calls me that from now on.

'I suggest that you get back in touch with us after you have talked to your mother,' Dad says kindly.

I think that's really big of him. I'd tell her to get lost if it was me. But my parents aren't like that. Mum manages a polite smile as she says, 'Tell your mother she is very welcome to come here to see us. And if she does we will discuss everything calmly and sensibly.' Her voice is very controlled and gentle, but I can see from the set of her mouth that she is really upset.

'I don't know why you didn't tell us about this

when you first came here, instead of pretending to be friends with us,' Ed blurts out, his voice loud and angry. 'You got in with us so you could snoop around the house looking for those stupid letters, that's right, isn't it?' he asks. Then he adds dismissively, 'You must be a bit touched. No one in their right mind keeps letters for twenty years. If Dad kept all his correspondence we wouldn't be able to get through the door for piles of paper. Doesn't your mother get any mail?'

'Those letters were really special,' Ally says. I can see she is hurt by Ed's reaction.

'Well, I think your mother wants to move on and get herself a life if she's still rereading her teenage love letters after all this time,' Nell says. 'And Ed is absolutely right. If you want to know who your father is, you should have approached us properly and been open about it.'

The twins always gang up together in times of trouble—which is a phenomenon I know well. But I can see that Ally is taken aback by them both putting the boot in—they are coming at her from both sides like a pair of terriers after a rat.

'It was very underhand of you to move in on us. Ed and I were really taken in,' Nell continues waspishly. 'In fact, the only person who realized what you were up to was our little Alice. And she'd worked the whole thing out. She's been playing detective and even knows where your mother is staying.'

I get the feeling that Nell enjoys telling Ally that she has been rumbled—and by me of all people.

Everyone turns to look at me. Mum and Dad both stare at me anxiously—as if they are worried I might keel over after such an unaccustomed bout of cleverness. Nell is looking smug: if she couldn't solve the mystery then at least her little sister could. Poor Ed is still upset. Ally turns and scowls at me, as if everything is my fault. And I suppose in a way it is. If I hadn't lied and got her into the party everything might have been completely different.

Thankfully, at that moment there is a knock on the door. 'I think this is Sam,' I say in a relieved tone.

I open the door but before Sam can come in Ally pushes past me, flounces over to her car, and drives off.

Ed and Nell insist on taking me and Sam down to the pub. I suppose they feel that Mum and Dad need a bit of time on their own to discuss what has happened. Ed buys us ginger beer and we play pool. We laugh and joke and lark around, and none of us even mentions Ally's name. It's as if she never existed. It's very strange.

When we get back to the house Dad says it's too late for Sam to cycle. He puts Sam's bike in the back of the Land Rover and takes him home. I have a bath and get into bed.

I am woken out of a deep sleep by a series of crashes. I stare into the darkness, paralysed by shock. It's a terrible noise, like a rocket attack. Mabel is going berserk. I want to leap out of bed and run downstairs and comfort her but I can't move. I am too scared.

Normally I love thunderstorms but this doesn't sound like thunder. It is a noise so harsh and loud that I can't identify it. It sounds cruel, whatever it is, and it is right outside my window, so close that I flinch at each crash.

'Are you all right, Alice?' Nell asks. I have been cowering under the covers, trying to block out the noise, so I hadn't realized that she had come into my room. She pulls the pillow away from my face.

'What's happening? What's that terrible racket?' I ask with a sob.

Nell takes my hand. 'Someone is up on the crag throwing stones at the greenhouses. It is the sound of breaking glass that you can hear. Come on down to the kitchen. There's nothing we can do. Dad has phoned the police. He was all for racing up to the crag but Mum won't let him go, she says we've got to sit tight. She's making a hot drink. Come on, don't cry any more.'

Mum wipes my face with kitchen roll as if I am a little kid, sits me in a chair and makes me hot chocolate. Even though the night is warm I am shivering and I hold the warm mug gratefully. Mabel stops barking and comes and puts her head on my knee to comfort me. Really it's me who should be comforting her. I am such a coward!

'Don't be frightened, Alice,' Mum says, giving me a hug. 'It sounds awful with all the glass breaking, but it's only drunks walking back from the pub with nothing better to do than throw stones around.' She adds calmly, 'We've phoned the police. But by the time they get here whoever it is will have run off. And there's very little chance of finding anyone in the woods in the dark.'

There is one final volley of stones, a few more panes of glass clunk down. There can't be much left out there still standing.

Dad goes over to the door and starts to unbolt it.

'Don't go out,' Mum says, suddenly agitated. 'There's nothing you can do. You've got no chance of catching them.'

'If they are drunk they won't be able to run very fast,' he says bitterly. I get the feeling that he isn't totally convinced by Mum's version of events. 'I might be able to see who it is,' Dad says. I can see that he is furious—really angry.

'There's no point,' Mum says quickly. 'And it's dangerous. Gramps is insured. The police know about it and they've said they'll check the village and the main road. Just leave it, Rob.'

As if to prove her right about it being dangerous there is one final crash: as if the person on the crag has found one last stone and chucked it for good measure.

'There, I told you it wasn't safe,' Mum says. 'Vandals don't care who they hurt,' she adds. There are two bright spots of colour in her cheeks. She is keeping cool but I can see that she is close to tears.

I meet Nell's eyes. No one speaks. I suppose no one wants to state what is glaringly obvious. There is one person who bears us enough of a grudge to vandalize the greenhouses. But none of us dare to say her name. I think about Garden Heaven and the break-in at Bradley Road and I start to shiver so violently that I slop my hot chocolate down my pyjamas.

'Come on, pet,' Dad says, handing me more kitchen roll. 'They've gone now. Don't be scared. All the doors are locked. You are quite safe.'

The night seems achingly silent after all the noise. I go back to bed. I hear the police arrive. I hear them leave. I listen to the tick-tock of my clock. I can't sleep and neither can I bear to be alone any more. I feel I must have company. For a while I toy with the idea of going down to the kitchen and curling up with Mabel in her basket. I know I would get the warmth and comfort I need from her. But I am nervous about going downstairs. Also I need someone to talk to.

Stealthily I make my way to Nell's room. I can hear her talking on her phone, her voice low and urgent. So I tap on her door and push it open.

'Look, I've got to go. Little sister is here, we're all still a bit upset,' Nell says. Her eyes are sad and her beautiful mouth is curved as if she might cry. And I don't think it's Gramps's greenhouses that are making her weep.

'Who was that?' I ask.

'Spence—if we can't argue face to face we have to do it by phone,' Nell says bitterly. 'What's the matter with you? You're not still blubbing, are you? Come on, there's nothing to be scared of. Whoever did it will be miles away by now.'

'I'm cold,' I mumble.

'You can't be cold. It's like being in the Sahara tonight. Anyway, come into bed and I'll give you a cuddle,' she says.

I slide in next to her. 'Your feet are cold,' she complains.

'Why are you and Spence fighting?' I ask.

'We are too different to get along. He wants things which I think are a waste of time and he thinks that I am over-ambitious and materialistic. They say opposites attract. Well, they may attract but the result is anarchy. I'm going to have to finish with him. He's doing my head in. I think it would be best to have a clean break before I go away to uni.'

'Isn't he going to uni too?' I ask.

'Oh no, he's dropping out. I've told him he's crazy . . .' Her voice wobbles.

We are both silent for a while, both lost in our thoughts of Spence. 'Now, what's the matter with you? Is it Ally?' Nell asks.

'Yes,' I whisper. 'Nell, what are we going to do if she is our half-sister? She's a complete nutter.'

'It will be absolutely terrible if she is our sister. Frankly it doesn't bear thinking about. There's no way Ed and I are ever going to forgive her. We feel totally used. And you are right, she is weird . . . and dangerous . . . I wouldn't be surprised if it was her up on the crag tonight throwing stones at us. She's a bit wild. And if, by some misfortune, she's related to us I suppose we will have to bear it as best we can and have as little to do with her as possible,' she adds.

'Yes,' I say in a quavering voice. 'Nell, you don't think Mum and Dad will get divorced or anything like that, do you?'

'NO!' Nell says. 'If Mum was going to be jealous of Polly whatever-her-name-is she would have got it out of her system by now. After all, Dad married Mum and not Polly. And look how hard he's always worked so she could have a career. They are rock-solid. Look on the bright side. Ally is nearly twenty—she'll soon be an adult—and hopefully she'll grow up a bit. So, even if she is Dad's offspring, she won't be hanging around him too much. If she was a little kid it might be different. It's just bad luck she's such a strong personality and that she has the same name as you. Has that upset you?'

'Yes, I think it has a bit. I feel as if she's trying to steal my identity and my family.'

'That's just soft,' Nell says, giving me a hug. 'I mean, I know Ed and I tease you a bit, but you are our baby sister. No one else could ever take your place, could they?'

'I suppose not,' I say. 'Nell, when are you going to tell Spence that you are finished?'

'Tomorrow morning, first thing—I'm setting my alarm clock so I can go into work early and see him.

191

There's no point in delaying things. I've made up my mind,' she says.

'He'll be upset, won't he?' I say.

'Yes, and so will I,' Nell says swiftly. 'But sometimes the sharpest cut is the kindest. He'll be leaving for America soon and I'll be going to uni so we'll both have things to take our minds off it.'

'He's going to America?' I whisper. 'How long is he going to America for?'

'I don't know,' Nell says a bit irritably. 'Neither does he. That's one of the problems. It's like he's on a different planet to me.'

'That's because he's artistic—he's a songwriter. He has the mind of a poet. I suppose he experiences the world differently to the rest of us,' I say.

Nell sighs. 'Honestly, he would have been better off going out with someone of your age. You seem to understand him far more than I do. I think it's just plain dopey of him to want to go traipsing off to the States with no money and only a couple of A levels to his name. He'll end up living in a trailer and washing dishes for a living.'

'Maybe he'll be happy doing that. He'll probably write beautiful songs about it,' I say sadly.

'Yes, well. That may be so. But he'll have to do it without me,' Nell says briskly. 'I've had enough of scrimping and scraping. I've spent my life having no money and being the poor relation when we go to Italy. I don't want to drop out. I want to be successful and rich.'

'I'm sure you will be,' I say.

Nell gives me another hug. 'Go back to bed and go to sleep. Don't worry about Ally. I don't think she's our sister. She was always moaning about her father—the one who has the sci-fi job in America. Evidently he's really strict. She's just fed up with him and thinks it would be great to have a different dad. She's an awful drama queen.'

'OK,' I say. Then, before I can help myself, I add: 'Nell, you won't be hard on Spence when you tell him, will you?'

'No. I'll try to be kind. I'll try to remember he has the mind of a poet,' she says wryly.

Chapter 18

I go back to bed and go to sleep. And I dream of Spence. We are lost on a mountainside in thick fog and, even though I call out his name again and again, I can't find him. When I wake up I'm crying. Today it will be over between him and Nell and he will go off to America—and then I will never see him again. The enormity of this fills my mind—I can't think of anything else, not even about Ally, or Gramps's greenhouses, or any of the terrible things that have happened.

I look at my clock and realize that it's really late. I try to ring Sam but his phone is off. No one but Gramps has sent me a message. I feel really left out: everyone but me is busy. And everyone here will have gone off to work or college so I know I must get up and go down to see Mabel but it takes all my energy to get out of bed. I feel a million years old.

Brilliant sunshine is pouring through my window, showing the threadbare patches in the carpet and throwing the muddle in my room into grotesque relief. Today—even though my heart is breaking—I must get my room tidied.

I shower and get dressed in shorts and T-shirt and make my way downstairs. Nell is there. Her eyes are all puffy and I can tell straight away that she's been crying. 'I've had to come home. I can't work!' she says dramatically.

'What's happened?' I cry in alarm.

'Spence is on a day off. So I went round to his house this morning. We had an awful row. I think it would be best if I don't see him again. It's pointless to keep on punishing us both. Neither of us can change.'

'Is he very upset? Did he take it very badly?' I ask forlornly.

'Yes, he did,' she says. 'Really, I would have thought that he would have seen it coming.' She sighs and adds: 'Alice, will you do me a favour? I need to give some CDs and books back to him. If I drive you to his house will you go in and hand them over? I can't face seeing him again. There really is no point.'

'Me?' I say in horror. I can feel my stomach turning, as if I am in a lift that is moving too fast. 'Me?'

'Go on, Alice, please.' Then seeing my reluctant face she adds: 'Spence really likes you. He's always going on about what a great kid you are. He says you are a "one off".'

'Is that in any way a compliment?' I ask, bemused.

'Yes, of course it is! It means you are original. Please say you'll do it. It will only take you a minute. And it will give you a chance to say goodbye to him. I always thought you really liked him,' she adds, giving me a searching look.

'OK. I'll do it,' I say grimly, turning my head away

from her. She is already talking about him in the past tense. As if he's died, or gone away to some far off distant place, and we'll never see him again. And it brings it home to me—that is what's going to happen. This really is the end. I may never see him again.

Nell sorts out a cardboard box full of stuff and puts it on the kitchen table. 'Is all this his?' I ask. I just manage to curb my curiosity and stop myself from peering inside the box.

'Some things are presents he bought me. I don't want to keep them,' she says.

'You've really got it in for him, haven't you?' I say bleakly. If Spence gave me a present I'd treasure it for the rest of my life.

'I just don't know why he let me go on for so long making plans about us being together, when all the time he had this stupid notion of going to America in the back of his mind. It makes me look such a fool. I don't understand him. He says he wants to find himself. But honestly, he sounds so flaky when he talks about it.'

'OK, OK, spare me the gory details,' I say, putting my hands over my ears because I don't want to listen to her saying mean things about Spence. It really hurts me. 'I'm sorry I asked. Let's get going. It's as hot as hell. Gramps sent me a text saying it's going to rain today. He says he can smell it. I hope he's right.'

We drive in silence. The car is stuffy and almost unbearably warm. I try to imagine icebergs and skiing holidays and freezing cross-country runs in November when the cold chaps your legs, but sweat slides down between my shoulder blades and makes my palms sticky.

It seems like divine retribution that I should be the one sent in to see Spence for the last time. I am acutely aware that I mustn't make a fool of myself. I don't want to be waking in the middle of the night for years to come remembering something really stupid that I'd said to him.

We drive through a modern estate. I stare at all the gardens and wonder how the people who live here have managed to keep them looking so immaculate with bright green grass and flowering bedding plants. We've had a hosepipe ban virtually all summer. 'Do you think they all get up in the middle of the night to water their gardens?' I ask Nell, but she ignores me.

Eventually we pull up in front of a detached house. 'This is it,' Nell says. Her hands are gripping the steering wheel so tightly her knuckles are white. I feel nervous too.

'It's a huge house, isn't it?' I say uncertainly.

'Get a move on then, Alice. It's too hot to park. I'll drive around the block.' Nell is irritable now.

I grab the cardboard box and run up the path which leads to Spence's front door. The house really is massive, much bigger than our terrace in Bradley Road, or even Gramps's old stone house. But it has a neglected air. The hedge needs trimming and this lawn certainly hasn't been watered all summer—it is the colour of beaten earth. The front door could do with a coat of varnish and some of the curtains are still drawn.

I have to lean on the bell for ages before Spence opens the door. His face is tight with misery and his eyes are red. I try not to stare. He looks much worse than Nell. The thought of him crying squeezes my heart until I am breathless.

'I've got some things for you, from Nell,' I whisper.

I hold out the box, but he moves away from the door and says, 'Come on in then, Alice.'

I walk in. He takes the box from me and says, 'Come along to the kitchen and let me get you a cold drink, you look hot.'

As I follow him I absorb every detail about his house. I am acutely aware that these are the last memories I will ever have of him. The house is clean but not homely. The rows of trainers in the porch are lined up neatly, like in a tidy changing room, but there aren't any flowers or pictures or personal touches. It seems a sad house. I don't know why I think that but I do.

Spence puts the box down on the table, opens the fridge, finds a carton of juice and pours some into a glass for me.

'Have a seat,' he says.

I sit down and put my hot hands around the cold glass of juice. 'Gramps says it's going to rain. He says he can smell it,' I say, and then I stop abruptly and bite my lip. I sound ridiculous. Talking about the weather at a time like this!

'Did Nell drive you over?' he asks. He's poured himself some juice but he's not drinking it. He's looking into the glass as if it's a crystal ball.

'Yes, she's driving around the block to keep cool.' I gulp my drink. 'I'll have to go,' I add.

'I had no idea she was so unhappy. It was a complete shock when she came here today.' To my horror his eyes fill with tears.

'I'm so sorry,' I say lamely.

'It seems that I can't lead the life I want and have Nell for a girlfriend. It's a hard choice to make.'

'Yes, I can see that,' I say.

'She's so clever, so intelligent, and yet there are some things she just doesn't understand,' he says. I don't reply. He carries on: 'My mother has met someone, she's planning to move to Scotland to be with him. It's freed me up. You know my father walked out soon after my brother, Brad, was born.'

I don't reply, but I meet his eyes, and he looks straight at me as he talks. 'My mother seemed to do nothing but cry and sleep for a year after my father left. I soon got really good at heating up bottles, changing nappies, and getting myself cereal to eat any time of the day or night when I was hungry.'

I drag my gaze away from him and stare at the kitchen walls. Anything to drive away the image of Spence as a little boy, sitting at this table in his pyjamas, eating rice crispies on a cold morning with no one to look after him. I want nothing more than to hug and kiss him and make the world perfect for him. I want him never to be cold or hungry or lonely ever again. I want so much for him to be happy. I glance back at his miserable face and teary eyes and feel as if my heart will break.

'My father wants me to go and stay with him for a while. He says he'll help me find work in the States. I think he knows he ducked out and left us in the lurch and he wants to make it up to me now. I just want . . .' He stops in mid sentence, as if explaining what he wants is suddenly too difficult for him.

'I understand,' I say quickly. 'You've always had responsibility and looked after everyone and now you want your life to be different. But I don't think Nell needs a lot of looking after, does she?' I add rather uncertainly. Maybe I haven't understood after all.

He shakes his head and says slowly, 'Nell thinks that dropping out is for losers—I can either conform to her ideals or get lost. She thinks you can get freedom only by making lots of money. But maybe when I'm a famous singer songwriter she'll change her mind. What do you think, Alice?' He gives me a bit of a grin, and I manage a weak smile.

'Hey, little sis, if I give you my dad's email address how about you and me keeping in touch?' He doesn't wait for me to reply. He is already reaching for the notepad and pen that are next to the telephone. 'We'll always be friends, won't we?' he adds.

He writes down the address and gives me the piece of paper. I fold it up really, really small and put it in the pocket of my shorts. 'I better go,' I say. And then I add in a rush, 'If I don't email you, it isn't because I don't like you or care about what happens to you. It's just . . .'

He's surprised. I see a little frown drawing his brows together. I add quickly: 'I do understand about the freedom thing. I know just what you mean. I'm sure Nell will understand too, in time.'

What I can't explain to him is that I understand his desire for freedom only too well. My own personal prison, and vision of hell, had appeared before my eyes as he wrote down his email address. I imagined myself rushing home from school every day, desperate to turn on the computer in case there was a message from him.

And all the time I would know in my heart of hearts that he wanted to keep in touch with me because he loves Nell—and any contact with her is better than nothing. I would spend my time living in the shadows . . . and I suddenly know that I don't want that . . . and that I am worth more than that.

'Ed is always on the web. I'm sure he'll email you loads and when he does I'll say hello,' I say quietly. This is a compromise. I imagine the emails—and the standard last line that I will ask Ed to include: 'Alice says "Hi" and sends her love.' Spence will never know how true that last part is.

'Yes, fine. I'd just like to know how you all are

and what you are doing,' he says stiffly. I have hurt his feelings. I wish I had the courage to tell him that I too need to be free. But I can't say anything because he never tried to make me fall in love with him. It was just something that happened.

When I step outside the front door the world has changed. I walk slowly to the car and get in. 'OK?' Nell asks, and I nod.

It is only when we are driving past all the immaculate gardens on the estate that I realize what has happened. The sun has gone in. The sky is now a dirty-grey colour. And a hot breeze has sprung up from nowhere and is twisting and tormenting all the leaves on the ornamental cherry trees. Even though there is no sun it seems hotter. And inside the stifling warmth of the car the humid air is like a weight on top of my head.

When we turn into the lane that leads to Gramps's house I see that the sky above the crag is now black and yellow, like a huge bruise. And the breeze is now a teasing wind, whipping dust and straw across the road. The weather is breaking—just like my heart.

Chapter 19

To my delight Gramps is sitting by the open kitchen door with Mabel at his feet. I rush over to give him a hug and a kiss. Nell makes an excuse and goes straight upstairs. I suppose she doesn't want Gramps to see that she's been crying.

'Our Jess has gone shopping so she dropped me off here,' Gramps says. 'I wanted to see the state of the greenhouses. What a mess. The whole lot will have to come down. Just as well there were no plants in there. What a fuss and a bother you've all been having,' he adds sympathetically. 'And just fancy that friend of yours turning out to be Polly's daughter. Sly puss for not telling us, don't you think?'

Gramps shakes his head and continues, 'It's a lot of nonsense the idea that she's your dad's daughter. Polly adored your nana. There's no way she wouldn't have come and told us if she had a little girl that was our granddaughter. And there was no reason in the world why she wouldn't have told your dad. You know how easy-going he is. As I recall there wasn't a harsh word between them. Your dad went to Italy for the summer and met your mum—and Polly went to America to work and came back with a new boyfriend. There were no hard feelings. Polly's a lovely lass and she was never backward at coming forward. Trust me—your nana and me would have known all about it.'

I give Gramps another hug and we talk about Mabel and the puppies and Gramps writes me a list of special food and supplements that Mabel needs.

'They'll be lovely pups whoever the father is,' Gramps says reassuringly. Then he adds, 'I'm glad to have a chance to talk to you on your own, Alice. I wanted to tell you my news. I'm afraid I'm going to have to sell this old place. It's not just the damage to the greenhouses. That might have done me a bit of a favour because the insurance money will be a help. No, it's that there's no business any more with the superstore just up the road. Your mum has been such a help with clearing out all the junk I've been hoarding. And now that's done it'll have to go on the market, I'm afraid. I was worried you'd be upset,' he adds.

I am upset. I've always loved visiting Gramps—it's part of my childhood—and even living here hasn't been too bad. Even though there's only one bus an hour—and no one but Sam has taken the trouble to come out and visit me.

'I had hoped to start a new business, growing strawberries under polythene tunnels, and using the greenhouse for organic salad leaves. But I haven't the money to get it going,' Gramps says.

'What about the insurance money?' I ask.

'That'll just be a drop in the ocean, pet,' he says.

I feel as if things can't get any worse. Mum and Gramps without work. Spence going to America . . . But when Mabel starts to bark, and a flashy jeep pulls into the yard, I know that I have been tempting fate. Things can get worse—they just have!

I recognize the dark-haired woman who gets out of the jeep immediately. It's Polly Marshall. She's wearing a silky summer dress and dainty sandals. She doesn't look like a lady gardener—she looks like a fashion model. Trailing behind her, in dark glasses, black clothes, and scarlet lipstick, is Ally—looking more like a Dracula clone than ever.

I bolt upstairs to the bathroom because I really don't want to talk to them. I splash my face with cold water. And then I spend ages folding the towels and cleaning the bath. I tap on Nell's door and then open it. She is lying on the bed staring up at the ceiling. I tell her that Ally is here but she just shakes her head at me. No help there then . . .

Finally I make my way downstairs. And when I get into the kitchen I find Polly Marshall busy pouring out a pot of tea and putting biscuits on a plate—just as if she owns the place. I think she can see from my expression that I think this is a cheek.

She says hello to me, and how nice it is to meet me, and then adds with a little smile, 'Alice, you must excuse me making myself at home. I spent many happy hours here with your grandparents. I'm just making Pops . . . Mr Garvey,' she corrects herself quickly, 'a cup of tea. It's very cooling in the heat. Would you like one?'

'Thanks,' I mutter. Out of the corner of my eye I can see Ally looking sulky. It is strange: being here with her mother makes her seem like a little girl— as if in some odd way she has shrunk and become a child again.

'I've come to apologize to you all. I couldn't believe it when Ally told me she'd had a showdown with Rob about who her father is. It is so ridiculous. I'm sorry if it has upset you all.'

Ally's lower lip pouts even more.

Polly is rattling away—boy, can she talk! 'I've just signed for a house in Leeds. I've got a contract with YTV for a brand-new gardening programme. It's going to be called *Muck and Magic*. It'll be just your kind of thing, Pops,' she adds enthusiastically. 'Organic vegetables and how to get the most out of small gardens as well as programmes on patios and pots and balcony gardening. There'll be something for everyone. The only problem I've had is finding a co-presenter. I'm not the easiest person to work with,' she adds.

Out of the corner of my eye I see Ally pull a face and roll her eyes to heaven. If Polly sees this she ignores it completely as if Ally is a naughty toddler. Instead she turns to Gramps with a laugh and says, 'Now, what I really need is a mature man who knows about practical gardening.'

· 'Ah, I get the picture, same old Polly,' Gramps

says teasingly. 'He'll be the muck and you'll be the magic.'

Polly Marshall laughs again. She and Gramps have obviously been good friends in the past. I try to study her without making it too obvious. She is thinner than she appears on TV and she does have a cheerful manner. I try to imagine her and my dad when they were young and in love and fail completely.

'Now, you'd be perfect for it,' she says to Gramps, her eyes narrowing speculatively. 'Have you thought of branching out into the media? Or are you still very busy here?'

I sense Ally tensing up. I bet she's terrified that Polly will get to hear about the greenhouses and come to the same conclusion as everyone else—that Ally was responsible.

'The garden centre has come to the end of its life, I'm afraid. We've had a bit of vandalism that's the last straw,' Gramps says carefully. 'I am going to be looking for something else to do,' he adds. 'But I'm not television material, pet. I'm an old wreck—well past my sell-by date.'

Polly smiles at him and says, 'Rubbish. Have you ever done a screen test? Would you come through to Leeds and meet my producer? It's an easy schedule. The money would be good. Would you be interested, Pops? Oh, please say you'll give it a try. You're just what my silver-top ladies and I need!'

'Get away, what nonsense,' Gramps says, laughing. But I think he is flattered to be asked. He is very old but he does have lovely white hair and a craggy face full of laughter lines. I think he's wonderful and it's obvious that Polly thinks so too, which makes me feel warmer towards her. Also it's difficult not to get swept up in her enthusiasm.

'I can't walk without two sticks until I get my blasted knee sorted. After the op I've got to rest it completely,' Gramps says. 'You couldn't have a gardener in a wheelchair.'

'Of course you could be in a wheelchair,' Polly says bossily. 'In fact, it could be seriously inspirational. We could do an entire programme on raised gardens and great stuff like that. Anyway, we could soon prop you up behind a table. I'd do all the running around. You'd just be there for decoration and to give the series a bit of gravitas. Now, just say you'll come to Leeds and talk about it. Please . . . I'm not asking for more than one little trip to Leeds and an informal chat,' she says, tilting her head and smiling at him.

'Ah well,' Gramps says with a smile. 'Just one little trip to Leeds, is it? You've learnt patience at last, Polly, my girl. One step at a time—that's not how you used to be at all.'

Polly laughs. 'No, I was always very impatient, wasn't I? Always rushing at life and grabbing it with both hands.'

Ally is staring into space as if she is meditating. Boredom radiates out of her like a force field. She was very different when she thought Gramps was her grandfather. Now she is acting as if he's a boring old man talking to her boring mother. I wish I could slap her face. It would make me feel so much better. Instead I gulp down my tea and wish they would leave.

But Polly is still talking. 'I really wanted Ally to apologize to Rob and Sophia in person,' she says. 'When do you expect them back? I raced over as soon as I found out. I am so cross with Ally. We may both dislike Gus, my ex-husband, but unfortunately we can't re-write history,' she adds with a little smile. She seems so confident and bubbly, and far too nice to be Ally's mother. I can't imagine her reading Dad's old letters and crying.

'No one is the least bit bothered about it,' I say loudly and clearly. 'It's all been completely forgotten about. I'll tell them you called by, but there really is no need to worry at all.'

I am desperate to get rid of them both. Much as I like Polly I don't want her to find out how bad things are for us. How Mum hasn't got a job and Dad is working too hard. I can tell by the jeep and her understated, elegant clothes that she is making serious money.

I glance at Ally and force a really sickly grin. 'It was an easy mistake to make, wasn't it? How is your gran, by the way?' I add. I have the satisfaction of seeing a moment of panic in Ally's eyes. She doesn't reply. I'm not surprised.

'Does your mother still live up here?' Gramps asks Polly.

'Good grief no—she remarried and moved to Spain years ago. She leads a completely hedonistic lifestyle: one long round of golf, gin, and sunbathing.'

'So is it Ally's other granny who lives up here?' I ask politely. I am enjoying myself. Ally is looking so uncomfortable. Her face is white and sweaty. It serves her right for being such a liar.

Polly smiles and says, 'Ally's other grandmother lives in New York. And she does nothing but parties, shopping, and holidays. Ally's just been over to stay with her and had a ball. What it is to be the rich retired,' she adds with a laugh.

'Well, it's very nice to have two grannies who are so happy, isn't it?' I say. I don't add that it's better than being old and infirm and in hospital—which is the fate of the fictitious granny that Ally has yakked on about all summer. I can see by the sick look on Ally's face that I've scored a hit and she's terrified I'm going to blow her cover. The truth is that I can't be bothered now I have the upper hand. I am much more interested in this amazing job opportunity for Gramps. I feel very kindly towards Polly—I think she's a bit of a star. I don't want to upset her.

Polly gives me a lovely smile, as if she thinks I am charming. And I smile back. Then she turns back to Gramps. 'I'm going to Leeds tomorrow for a meeting with my producer. How about coming along for the ride and a spot of lunch?' she says to Gramps.

He laughs. 'Just a meeting, I'm not promising any more than that.'

They swap telephone numbers and Gramps tells Polly where Auntie Jess lives. It is only after the jeep has driven off that I realize that Ally didn't say a single word during the whole visit. What a change!

'Now, Alice,' Gramps says, 'when are you going to take this boyfriend of yours out for a meal and trip to the pictures, to say thank you to him for helping in the shop?'

'He's not my boyfriend,' I say. 'He's just a friend. I'll ring him later.'

I'm desperate to talk to Sam. I've got so much to tell him about Ally. But I don't feel I can call him up and ask him out on a date. It seems so silly after all the time we've spent together. But I am very aware of the fact that I turned him down flat when he asked me to be his girlfriend—and he's never tried again. And why should he when I have spent the entire summer being in love with Spence? But now Spence is leaving. And I am free. But what can I say to Sam? Sorry, I've been a fool . . . I've changed my mind . . . It was you I was in love with all along only I couldn't see it? I know now that I have been in love with him, and in love with a dream, all at the same time. I can see it clearly now—but I don't think I could explain it to anyone—it would be so complicated and difficult.

'Ring him now,' Gramps insists. 'And ask him out. Let him know what a lucky lad he is,' Gramps adds with a grin, handing me his phone. 'Go on. Take it outside if you don't want me to listen. Only I'm not going home until you've asked him. It's a debt of honour on my part,' he jokes. 'The two of you put in so many hours and did so much work. I must at least treat you to a night out if you really won't have any wages. Come on, Alice, love. I've got my pride. I'm not a charity case yet.'

'No, you're not! And when you become a TV star you can treat us to lots of nights out,' I add, giving him a hug. 'It is exciting, isn't it?' I say, but he just laughs.

'Come along. I'll only go to see this producer fella if you ring your lad,' Gramps bargains.

'Oh, all right,' I say meekly. 'I'd hate to be responsible for you missing out on a career in television.'

Anyway, if I am truthful, I am desperate to ring Sam. My hands shake a bit as I tap in his number; I have to hope Gramps doesn't notice. He'll think I'm such a drip. But as soon as I hear Sam's voice it all becomes surprisingly easy.

'Hi, Sam,' I say cheerfully. 'I've got loads to tell you. And Gramps has given me some money for us to go to the cinema and out for a meal. Are you free tonight?'

I am so relieved when he says that he'd love to go out that I would have rung off right then. But, as usual, Sam is super competent and arranges tickets and buses.

By the time I get off the phone I am irrationally happy and my heart is singing. 'There,' Gramps says with satisfaction. 'That's a job well done.'

Auntie Jess arrives to collect Gramps and Nell comes downstairs to say 'Goodbye'. She's washed her face and put lipstick on—she looks like her old self again.

'It's still so hot,' she complains to Gramps. 'I thought you said it was going to rain.'

'It'll be here before long, mark my words,' Gramps promises.

We go outside with them—it's a relief to be out of the house. The heat is terrible. Even though there is no sun the air is hot like a blast from a furnace. The sky above the crag is now purple and heavy like over-ripe fruit. And a storm wind is making the trees in the dark wood thrash and moan. It is as if the world is in pain and convulsing.

'It's coming right enough. Just look at those clouds. They're near enough black. We're going to have a right good downpour,' Gramps says with satisfaction. 'It'll clear the air.'

We stand and wave goodbye to them. When the car is out of sight I turn to Nell and say, 'Polly says that Ally is definitely not Dad's daughter. I don't think Ally will ever come near us again. It was very strange seeing her here today. It was as if all the fight had gone out of her.'

'What a relief,' Nell says with a sigh. She looks up at the sky and adds, 'And what a relief that it is going to rain at long last . . . How wonderful. Cool clean rain . . . Just what we need to wash away the dust of the summer.' She wipes the sweat from her face with the back of her hand and says with a little laugh, 'Come on, Alice. Let's get our swimming things on and run around the garden, like we used to when we were little.'

'Suppose someone sees us,' I say uncertainly.

'There's no one to see. Come on, quick,' she shouts, and she grabs my arm and pulls me inside. 'Let's get changed and run outside before it starts raining. It will be such fun . . .'

We race each other up the stairs—yelling like a pair of mad things. From high above the crag comes the first ominous rumble of thunder and it spurs us on. I drag my clothes off and throw them on the floor. Then I pull on my bikini. I meet Nell on the landing and we hoot and holler together as we run downstairs.

Mabel sits in her basket and watches us with a bemused expression in her eyes. And as we dance across the kitchen, chanting a silly nursery rhyme about pitter-patter raindrops, she curls up and puts her tail over her face. Poor Mabel doesn't like thunderstorms. Nell and I love them.

The scorched grass of the lawn is hot under my bare feet and the air is so warm that it is like being wrapped in a blanket. Nell and I stand in the middle of the garden holding hands. We have been singing and shrieking like savages but we are suddenly silent, with our heads thrown back staring at the sky. We are waiting for our cue. We are going to be washed clean from the dust and the heat, from being in love with the wrong person, from Spence, from Ally, from fear.

I am scared to blink in case I miss a single second of the build-up to the storm. It is so thrilling! There is another long rumble and then a flash of lightning. We wait, poised like two arrows ready to be loosed. And then slowly the first heavy drops of rain start to fall. They are the size of ten pence pieces and unexpectedly cold. It's an awful shock to feel them, sharp as pinpricks, on my bare shoulders and upturned face.

Our moment has arrived: Nell opens her mouth and lets out a piercing scream of exhilaration. I follow suit. And then we leap and jump around as if demented. The roar of the thunder mingles with our shouts until the cacophony seems to gain a life of its own. The noise rises like smoke through the trees and echoes around the hunched rocks and stones of the crag—so that myriad unearthly voices scream back at us in the rapidly-fading light.

I fling back my sodden hair and stare up at the crag and the jumping stones. They are black as a night sky, glistening in the rain. They look sinister and ugly—like monsters—but I'm not afraid. There's no one up there any more. It is deserted: no campsite, no red dress, no one spying, no stones crashing down on our family life.

Then my screams turn to long whoops of happiness. She's gone! Now we are nothing to her and she is nothing to us. She's gone and she'll never come back to haunt us. *I am the only Alice.*

Julia Clarke trained as a teacher at Goldsmiths' College, London, and as an actress at the Guildford School of Acting. She worked in educational theatre until her children were born when she started writing novels, short stories, and articles. Six novels for adults have been followed by several novels for teenagers. Julia lives on a farm in North Yorkshire with her husband, son, and daughter. In 1999 she was awarded an MA(Dist.) in creative writing from the University of Leeds. *The Other Alice* is her fifth novel for Oxford University Press.